Dinah Maria Mulock Craik

An Unknown Country

Dinah Maria Mulock Craik

An Unknown Country

ISBN/EAN: 9783337220112

Printed in Europe, USA, Canada, Australia, Japan

Cover: Foto ©Andreas Hilbeck / pixelio.de

More available books at **www.hansebooks.com**

AN UNKNOWN COUNTRY

BY THE AUTHOR OF

"JOHN HALIFAX, GENTLEMAN"

ILLUSTRATED BY FREDERICK NOEL PATON

NEW YORK

HARPER & BROTHERS, FRANKLIN SQUARE

1887

CONTENTS.

PART I.

FROM ANTRIM TO CUSHENDALL. . . . .

PART II.

CUSHENDALL AND CUSHENDUN . . . .

PART III.

THE GIANT'S CAUSEWAY . . . . . .

PART IV.

LONDONDERRY. . . . .

PART V.

GWEEDORE . . . .

PART VI.

FROM GWEEDORE TO CARRICK . . . .

SUNRISE AT CARNLOUGH.
(*From a Drawing by* F. NOEL PATON.)

[See p. 36.]

LIST OF ILLUSTRATIONS.

	PAGE
MUCKISH AND THE LAKE AT ARDS .	*Frontispiece.*
SUNRISE AT CARNLOUGH	vii*
SHANES CASTLE, LOUGH NEAGH .	10
ROUND TOWER, ANTRIM .	26
THE WITCH'S STONE . . .	30
AT GARRON POINT . . .	35
COTTAGES NEAR GARRON TOWER .	37
WATERFALL AT GLEN ARIFF . .	65
FAIR HEAD IN FOUL WEATHER	70
TOMB OF THE FIRST LORD ANTRIM AT BONAMARGY	71
DUNSEVERICK CASTLE	74
A NOR'-EASTER	75

PAGE

LANDING-PLACE NEAR THE GIANT'S CAUSEWAY   78

THE PLEASKIN AND "GIANT'S EYE-GLASS" .   81

CARRICK-A-REDE BY MOONLIGHT 91

DUNLUCE CASTLE 103

THE GAP OF BARNES   123

RATHMULLEN   129

KILMACRENAN   132

HOLY WELL AT DOOAN   135

HORN HEAD 139

GWEEDORE GLEN 153

MOUNT ERIGAL, GWEEDORE   155

SKULL ISLAND   157

THE POISON GLEN 183

IN THE ROSSES   197

SALMON LEAP AT CARRICK   209

THE LAIR OF THE WHIRLWINDS   213

GLEN COLUMBKILLE   225

ST. COLUMBA'S CROSS 227

MALIN BAY 228

ONE MAN'S PATH—SLIEVE LEAGUE   230

AN UNKNOWN COUNTRY.

PART I.

FROM ANTRIM TO CUSHENDALL.

YES—it is a country as absolutely unknown to its two sister countries as if it were in the backwoods of America. And yet it is within twenty-four hours of London, the same of Edinburgh, and less than half that time of Dublin. A region so strangely beautiful in its desolation and isolation that, ever since I first saw it, in a passing glimpse fifteen years ago, it had rested on my mind, amid all the countries I have since travelled through, as a land quite peculiar, which I longed to revisit and investigate, to see if the second impression confirmed the first. So this year, in spite of its condition of political crisis and general social upheaval, foreboding—may Heaven avert them!— no end of troubles to come, I declared my intention of taking our annual holiday journey in the north of Ireland.

1

It was amusing to watch the mingled surprise and disapproval on my friends' faces. "Going to travel in Ireland! Are you not afraid of being shot? Do you expect to get anything to eat? Do you mean to live in a dirty cabin, with the pig—'the gentleman who pays the rint' (which he has not done lately)—for your companion; a turf fire, and no chimney to speak of? What can you possibly find in Ireland—especially the north of Ireland—worth seeing or worth writing about?"

So argued ordinary acquaintances; while some affectionate utilitarians, taking the usual friendly privilege of speaking their minds, declared unhesitatingly that it was the most quixotic project that ever was formed, even by an individual who is rather given to doing things which nobody else ventures to do, but which, to the great surprise of practical-minded critics, sometimes do actually succeed!

For six long months I answered these protests with a smiling silence, possibly rather aggravating; but what was the good of argument? I had deliberately made up my mind, settled my proceedings, faced my difficulties, and counted the cost of them all.

First, as to being shot—which to the English mind seems the natural result of going to Ireland. An Irishman generally commits crimes from what he considers the highest of motives; though he will murder, he will seldom steal. I was sure that in these times, as in ancient days, of which Moore wrote in his immortal Irish melodies, four lone women—I had asked three kind girls to come and take care of me—might traverse Ireland from end to end and "feel not the least alarm." As to food, if we could get bread, butter, milk, and eggs *ad libitum*, and of the best kind, as I was informed would be the case, we should not starve; probably be better fed than I have been in many a grand foreign hotel. For the rest — is not nature always worth seeing, and human nature worth writing about? The only test is the eye that sees and the heart which takes in and " sets down naught in malice." And I knew my intent was good ; that I was doing nothing hastily, or selfishly, or su- perficially, for the mere object of " making a book."

Without presuming to come forward with any panacea for the ills of poor old Ireland, done to death for centuries with external nostrums, when her real cure lies within her- self, it struck me that a woman—only a woman—Irish by blood and English by education, old enough to possess a certain amount of experience as well as common - sense, especially the experience that one gets from travelling in foreign countries, and comparing them with one's own— might see things which cleverer people failed to see, and say things which less unbiassed people dared not say, concern- ing a country which is so little appreciated because so little known. For with nations, as with human beings, " love is the fulfilling of the law." You must go to them with an open heart, and at least try to love them, else you will never understand them.

To this end I had one advantage—that of being abso- lutely non-political. Ladies' Land Leagues, Primrose Hab- itations, and Female Suffrage Societies are to me equally obnoxious. I do not care two straws whose hand steers the national ship, provided it is a strong, steady, and honest hand. If it should please Providence and the enlightened British nation to grant my sex a vote, I am afraid I shall give mine, irrespective of party, to the best man, the most capable and well-educated man, and the truest gentleman, whether he be Radical or Conservative, the son of a duke or of a blacksmith.

Also, I detest all religious warfare—the creed not of love but of hatred, into which, alas! Christianity has been corrupted, until it is made by many to consist, not in holding fast your own faith, but in trying to tear limb from limb—spiritually, sometimes bodily—every one whose faith is different from yours. I believe that men of all faiths— nay, even those poor souls who have no faith at all — ought to live together in brotherly peace, neither meddling with nor condemning each other; sure that God can manifest himself through the righteous of every creed, or no creed; and that, however we may hate one another, he hates no man—except the bigot and the hypocrite.

It seems to me, in all humility, that a woman who thought thus, and was not afraid or ashamed to say so, was not the worst person to go to that "most distressful country," and tell what she saw there to other countries, whose crass ignorance on the subject is often comical, sometimes pathetic, and always harmful. There is no condemnation so severe as that of a person who knows absolutely nothing of what he condemns.

To this long preamble — but not longer than was necessary—I will only add that I started with the firm resolve not to trust to second-hand evidence, but to see all I could with my own eyes, and hear it with my own ears; since in Ireland, as in many other places, the most difficult thing in the world to get at is a fact; and when you have got it, you generally hear it twisted into so many opposite versions that you are led to question its existence at all.

So we started, a party of three, with power to add to our number. Not, I confess, without some misgivings, and a sensation akin to that of Saint Paul, when he went to Rome, not knowing what things should befall him there. Still, on the whole, we had a good courage, strengthened by three pleasant days at bonny Carlisle; though it ebbed a little as we swept on to Stranraer, followed by sheets of driving rain, and a wind — oh, that ominous wind! It haunted us all through the night in a dreary hotel, and when our eyes opened to a pleasant dawn, there it was, shaking the trees of a churchyard opposite. We could not stay —we felt bound to go, stormy though the weather might be. So, lured by the brilliant sunshine and the smiling, deceitful sea, we found ourselves, at seven in the morning, in the deck-cabin of the Larne steamer, waiting for the hapless passengers who had been travelling all night. They came, a forlorn-looking troop, and a few minutes afterwards we set sail for the "Island of Saints," as Ireland used to be called.

Alas! not now. The first thing we heard—in talking with two bright-faced Irish girls who had come from Oban the day before, and were going on to Dublin that night, yet seemed as cheery and as neat as if they had just stepped out of a bandbox—was about the continued Belfast riots. They told us a train had been stopped at Portadown, and Miss Minnie Palmer, the actress, had been shot at as her carriage was passing through the town. (N.B.—These "facts" were considerably modified afterwards, as were many others before we left Ireland.) Nevertheless, the girls did not seem at all afraid, but chatted gayly as we sailed down the smooth lough, which extends for a few peaceful miles before reaching the open sea. They took everything easily — riots included — speculating as to whether they should "see any fighting" as they passed through Belfast, and maintaining with us an animated conversation on Irish affairs, which, as we afterwards daily learned, is just now like playing a game of whist, in which your one thought is to discover your neighbor's hand and conceal your own.

At last the breezy day, where bright sunshine added insult to injury, forced us all into silence. To be "rocked in the cradle of the deep" may sound well enough in poetry, but there is some reason in the angry protest of the man who declared that, had he been present at the Creation, he would have advised that the world should be made "without such a thing as an island."

That unfortunate island! How lovely it looked as we touched Larne, and saw thence the shining half-circle of Belfast Lough, one of the finest harbors in the three kingdoms. As smiling and kindly was the welcome — though a stranger's—to me and my two English girls, who had never set foot in Ireland before, and who, when left here in bene-

ficent charge for three days, while I went on to Antrim,
bade me good-bye with a wistful earnestness, as if I were
setting them adrift in a rudderless boat on their way to
the North Pole, or somewhere equivalent. (They told me
afterwards that those three days were full of pleasant-
ness from beginning to end.)

The line from Larne to Antrim follows the usual plan
of Irish railways—of making the journey as long and as
roundabout as possible. Still it was not wearisome. A
sunshiny sea on one hand, and a smiling country on the
other. Cultivated country; acres of potatoes, beans, and
oats, with cottages here and there—not cabins, but cottages,
well built, roofed, and glazed; often covered with creepers,
and brightened by pretty little gardens full of flowers.
Could this be the land of terror and misrule? Was it possible to believe that a few miles off there was street-fighting
hand to hand, between fellow - Christians, who read the
same Bible, wherein is written, "Whoso hateth his brother
is a *murderer*?"

English people never can understand that Ireland is
peopled by two races — nay, by several races, as distinct
from one another as the Cornishman or East Anglian is
from the Northumbrian or the Lowland Scot. So that *vox
populi* by no means implies a combined voice, and the
phrase "So Irish!"—alas, too often an opprobrious adjec-
tive—includes types of character as opposite as the poles.
Here, for instance, on this Antrim coast, which was populated almost entirely by immigration from Scotland, the
faces, the manners, nay, the very accent, were so strongly

Scotch that it was difficult to believe one's self on the
western, rather than the eastern, shore of the Irish Channel.
Still more difficult—except when one thought of the Cove-
nanters, whose blood, traceable through generations, yet lin-
gers here—was it to realize that an industrious, well-to-do,
thriving, peaceful population, should give way to such a
Cain-and-Abel madness.   Which yet had a sort of prudent
method in it—for a friend told us, laughing at our fears,
that Belfast was "quite quiet in the daytime;" that the
gentlemen went up to business, and the ladies to do their
shopping, only taking care to come away before 6 P.M.,
"when the fighting began."   It was extraordinary how
little people living on the spot seemed to trouble themselves about a state of things which had seemed so dreadful
to us at a distance.

"We'll not talk about it, since we can't mend it," was
the wise though sad conclusion that I and my hosts came
to on this heavenly day, when, as we drove through the
sleepy little town of Antrim, it seemed hardly possible to
believe there was beginning, within fifteen miles of us, that
civil war which, English newspapers declared, was already
inevitable.   "We do not get too many such days as this in
Ireland, even in summer" (it was the 17th of August, but
seemed full summer still); "let us not waste an hour, but
go direct to Shanes Castle."

My friends seemed to think I knew all about that place,
but in truth I was in a state of total ignorance concerning
Shanes Castle and the great Irish chieftains, the O'Neills, to
whom it belonged.   I had never even heard of the first

O'Neill, the Red Hand of Ulster, who, colonizing that
country by the usual means, invasion, heard his Viking
leader say that it should belong to the first man who
"touched land," and accordingly cut off his own left hand
and flung it ashore. The descendants of this hardy, if
rather savage, gentleman long lived at Shanes Castle, which
was destroyed by fire in 1816. The present inhabitants are
a family whose original name was Chichester. They have
built a desirable modern mansion; and are excellent people,
I was told, fulfilling all their social and domestic duties,
much respected in the county, and having nothing of the
wild O'Neills of old except the name.

A fierce race, indeed, these must have been, and their
doings and sufferings fill an important page in Irish history. I shall not attempt to lift it. Perhaps there is no
civilized country, except Italy, in which are kept up as in
Ireland the *vendettas* of generations; when decent, respectable modern men and women work themselves up into
hurricanes of rage over the wrongs of their great-great-
grandfathers centuries ago. To the phlegmatic Saxon all
this seems very foolish, and yet — well, I must not enter on
this subject. Let the O'Neills sleep!—as they do, soundly
enough—in a nettle-and-bramble-covered old burial-place,
to which we came by a green avenue — in all seven miles
long.

Shanes Castle is said to be the finest "place" in Ireland
—except the Marquis of Waterford's seat, Curraghmore.
Such masses of underwood, of flowering shrubs growing
half wild, and of majestic forest trees—Nature semi-culti-

SHANES CASTLE,
LOUGH NEAGH.

(From a drawing by F. NOEL PATON.)

vated. But in the burial-ground Nature is left all to herself—too much to herself, perhaps—for it was rather sad to have to scramble through a wilderness of thorns and briars, and broken headstones in order to read one of the latest inscriptions:

"*This vault was built by Shane M°Brien M°Phelim M°Shane M°Brien M°Phelim O'Neill, Esq., in the year 1722, for a burial-place to himself and family of Clanneboye.*"

Doubtless meant for Clandeboye, near Holywood, Belfast—the early home of the present Lord Dufferin, who has made himself much more noted than his name. But how that worthy "Esquire," who put his whole pedigree into *his* name, must have clung to his ancestral home, when he planned for himself and his descendants this gloomy tomb! where he and they are alike deserted and forgotten—for the present O'Neills bury their dead elsewhere. Still, could not they, who have made their garden, called the Rockery, into a perfect Eden of beauty, spare a little thought, time, and money to clear away the weeds from over their deceased collateral ancestors? It matters little, of course; we shall all sleep sound under any coverlet; yet if I were an O'Neill I should not like to see those nettles growing rampant over my forefathers' bones.

Scarcely a stone's-throw from this gloomy place we came out suddenly upon the glittering expanse of Lough Neagh, the largest lake in the three kingdoms, twenty miles long by fifteen broad, looking like an inland sea. Not a ship or a boat of any sort dotted its vast, smooth surface; its long, level shores—for there is not a mountain near— added to the sense of silent, smiling, contented desolation.

"See how we Irish throw away our blessings," said my companion, as we stood looking at the lovely sight. "In England such a splendid sheet of water would have been utilized in many ways, and made a centre of both business and pleasure. Factories would have sprung up along its shores; yachts, steamers, fishing-boats, would have covered it from end to end. Now, Moore's solitary fisherman, who is supposed to stray on its banks

‘ At the clear, cold eve's declining ’—

(probably bent on catching pullan, the only fish attainable
here)—might easily imagine he saw

‘ The round towers of other days,
In the wave beneath him shining.’ ”

“ But did he ? ” I was foolish enough to ask ; because
most fiction has a grain of fact at its core. “ Was there
ever anything curious seen at the bottom of Lough
Neagh ? ”

“ I have dredged it from end to end, and found many
submarine curiosities, but never a round tower or a king's
palace ! Even the fossilizing power which is said to be in
its waters I believe lies not in the lake itself, but in one of
its tributaries, the Crumlin river, which has probably the
same petrifying and preserving qualities that exist in bog.
At any rate, the fossil wood, which is often found in the
lough, is extremely beautiful.”

“ And there is really no record of submerged cities ? ”
said I, still craving after my pleasant fiction. “ The waters
must cover such an enormous surface, which was probably
dry land once.”

“ Yes. It is said that about A.D. 100 the river Bann
overflowed, and drowned a prince of Ulster with all his
kingdom. Or, if you prefer it, your own Caxton declared
that the prince and his people, being ‘ men of evyle lyving,’
opened a holy well which was always kept closed. A
woman, with her child, went to draw water ; the child cried,
she ran to it, leaving the well uncovered, when up welled

the waters, destroying the whole country—including the woman and child. This is said to have happened A.D. 65. So you can choose between two conflicting dates and tradi-tions, and please yourself, as you mostly can in all histories. But here's an undeniable 'fact'—the castle."

Not the original fortress, built by the first O'Neill on the shores of Lough Neagh, with the good right hand yet left to him, but the half-modern, half-mediæval one which was burned to the ground as late as 1816. Its ruins, pictu-resque and ivy-grown, showed what a fine building it must have been. I was shown "Lord O'Neill's safe"—a sort of cupboard in the enormously thick wall—still left standing in what had been an upper room. Also the black stone, once a carved head, fixed in the outer masonry, to which clings a tradition that when it falls the family of O'Neill will end.

Of course, they have a Banshee—all real old Irish families have. Not the modern Anglo-Irish, who came over with Edmund Spenser, Oliver Cromwell, or King James, but the true Celts. A friend, whose uncle was present at the burning of Shanes Castle, told me the story of it. Lord O'Neill—a bachelor—had a party of gay bachelor friends dining with him. In the midst of their jollifications fire broke out in a distant room. Nobody minded it much at first—nobody does mind evil in Ireland till too late to mend it—and then they inquired for the fire-engine. It had been carried off that very day a dozen miles, to destroy a wasp's nest in a cottage roof! So there was nothing for it but to remove the pictures, furniture,

and valuables—or as much of them as they could—and let
the castle burn. Lord O'Neill and his companions, who
must have been pretty sober now, sat on an old box and
watched it burn. With the lough and its waters only a
few yards off they yet could do nothing, unless it was to
curse their own folly in letting go the only means of safety
—the fire-engine. While they sat, helplessly gazing, my
friend's uncle always declared he saw, and several of the
other guests affirmed the same, a female figure, all in white,
stand, wringing her hands, and then pass and repass from
window to window of the burning house, in which they
were certain there was no living creature. Of course, it
was the Banshee of the O'Neills.

After this no one attempted to rebuild the old castle,
but a new one was planned close by, its foundation being
made of the enormous underground passages found in
many ancient fortresses; probably meant first as refuges
in war-time, and then as rooms for the servants, who must
have been treated little better than serfs, or brute beasts.

There are yet living, I was told, persons who remember
what their grandparents have said about the manners and
customs in these splendid abodes, Shanes Castle and Antrim
Castle; how the under-servants were never allowed to appear in sight of the family or guest; these tunnel-like
places being made that they might get out to the town or
elsewhere, unobserved by their superiors.

Doubtless the lower class were not pleasant to look at
then—no more than they are now—to "your honor" and
"her ladyship." The great gulf between gentry and com-

monalty is a relic of those barbaric days, which seem less
distant here than they do in England, where the constant
immigration of other races has brought about a wider
civilization. One can hardly enter into the mind of that
Lord O'Neill who, when his castle was burned, made these
underground vaults, dark, damp, and unwholesome, for his
servants — planning for himself an enormous dining-hall
and reception - room, the walls of which still stand, up
to the window-ledges. There money failed; the building
was stopped, the builder died. His wiser successor has
converted the old lord's stables into a comfortable
modern house, farther inland, and left both castles, the
ruined old one and the never-finished new one, to moulder
away in picturesque peace on the shores of lovely Lough
Neagh.

Not far from them is the before - mentioned garden
called "The Rockery," which contains rocks of the same
curious formation as the Giant's Causeway. Its fertility is
wonderful. Forests of rare ferns, lakelets covered with
water - lilies — only leaves, it was too late for flowers—
masses of gorgeous autumn plants, laid out in borders
and beds, made it a little nook of beauty. A *tropæolum,*
the finest I ever saw, climbed in crimson festoons over
the black basaltic wall. The old gardener was evidently
very proud of it.

"Sure, ma'am, I trained it all meeself. Her ladyship,
she said to me, 'John, ye must have planned it in the
night.' And bedad, ma'am, so I did. There's many a good
thing thought of in the night."

He showed us a garden-house built of "fogg"—*i.e.* moss —most cleverly, even artistically. "They calls me John Fogg, because I built a fogg-house; but there's a wran here, she's built her nest in that bit of basalt. Says I to them, 'That little wran can build a better house than John Fogg.'"

This man, with his bright eyes gleaming out of his queer, ugly, not too clean face, and wearing a coat and hat that any English gardener would have utilized for a scarecrow, yet spoke with intelligence, humor, nay, even poetry, and with a charming natural courtesy which your excellent stolid Saxon could never have attained to. Hodge would have touched his decent cap, and answered our questions with a "Yes, sir," and "No, sir," receiving the eleemosynary shilling with a civil "Thank 'ee, sir." But as to conversing with us, giving us his sympathy and claiming ours, imparting all sorts of information, and a good many of his individual opinions on quite extraneous subjects— finally parting from us with a politeness that formed an almost ludicrous contrast to his ugliness and his rags—I must confess that Paddy had the best of it.

But now the afternoon sun was slowly declining, and the lough growing misty, though smooth still—a glassy mirror spread beneath the cloudless sky.

"Yet Lough Neagh can be rough. I have seen the waves come rolling in on these shores almost like a sea tide. And though it is never more than forty-five feet deep anywhere, and its lack of mountains saves it from the gusts which make most inland lakes so dangerous, still there are days when no boat would venture out. Our winters are stormy, though mild—as you may see by the sort of vegetation here"—pointing to the large fuchsia bushes, almost trees, evidently the growth of many years. "Only once have I seen Lough Neagh frozen over—in 1880 —when I skated across it quite alone, to that point you see, twenty miles there and back."

A rather risky proceeding, I thought, for the father of a family, but for once I did not speak my mind, being absorbed in the large, calm beauty of this islandless lake.

"It has one island," my friend said, "though you can hardly see it; a tiny dot of about six acres, with pretty woods, and a round tower. We sometimes picnic there— Little Ram's Island, opposite Balinderry."

What strange flashes of remembrance come sometimes! Many, many years ago, I had heard at a concert—of which the singers are all dead, and probably most of the audience, except one or two old folks, who then were young—a lovely old Irish song:

> "'Tis pretty to be in Balinderry,
>   'Tis pretty to be in Aghalee,
> But 'tis prettier to be in Little Ram's Island
>   Courting under the ivy-tree.
>   Ochone! Ochone!
>
> "For often I roved in Little Ram's Island
>   Side by side with Phelimy Hyland;
> And still he'd court and I'd be coy,
> Though at heart I loved him, my handsome boy.
>   Ochone! Ochone!"

I never could understand that wailing "Ochone!" till—a

2

lifetime after—I heard the rest of the song, in a modern-
ized version, founded upon Bunting's collection. It is
about one Mary, who would never own her love for her
"handsome boy" till just before he left.

> " 'I'm going,' he sighed, 'from Balinderry,
>   Out and across the stormy sea,
>   And if in your heart ye love me, Mary,
>   Open your arms at last to me.'

She did:

> "And there in the gloom of the groaning mast,
>   We kissed our first and we kissed our last.

> " 'Twas happy to be in Little Ram's Island,
>   But now it's as sad as sad can be.
>   For the ship that sailed with Phelimy Hyland
>   Is sunk forever beneath the sea.
>   Ochone! Ochone!'"

That sweet, sad refrain! I could hear it as if it were
yesterday. And now, after forty-years, I had come in
sight of "Little Ram's Island" and "Balinderry."

"We must take you there. We will get a boat and
make an expedition to-morrow. It is at the farther end
of the lough, but we *will* manage it."

An Irishman can manage anything, when he has persistency as well as energy. So I smiled consent, and we
drove merrily home."

August 18. — Alas! fate, and his country's eccentric
climate, can conquer even an Irishman. Next morning it
rained—as only it can rain in the Green Island. When in
the afternoon it cleared, in the amazingly sudden way that

it does clear here, there was no hope for an expedition which would have involved about sixteen miles of hard rowing. It was too late for Little Ram's Island.

Instead, I proposed to go and see the church. We had been sitting talking over many things — which being political and ecclesiastical, I shall not refer to here, except to record two facts, which I afterwards heard confirmed by much extraneous evidence. The Irish Church, instead of suffering, has actually benefited by Disestablishment, since the cessation of state support has turned towards it the thoughtful benevolence of laymen and land-owners. Also, the Catholic priesthood of the north of Ireland are generally of a superior class, and the Catholic population is fully as trustworthy as the Protestant. Sometimes more so, since they have less of theological bitterness than the descendants of the Scottish immigrants, who were chiefly the narrowest type of Presbyterians.

"I have sat for fifteen years in your church, sir," said a parishioner of this kind, giving notice that he meant to quit it. "And all that time I never heard you preach a single Protestant sermon."

That is, a sermon which not merely attests one's own faith, but protests against the faith of everybody who thinks differently—which is a very general interpretation of the word "Protestant"—making the most conscientious of us feel sometimes as if we would rather be Catholics. I could not help recalling the words—too little recalled now!—

"*It was said of old, Thou shalt love thy neighbor and hate*

thine enemy. But I say unto you—" Do the good Protestants of Ireland ever pause to remember *what* was said,
and Who said it.

Antrim Church dates from the fifteenth century, but
the glass window over the grand pew—Lord Massereene's
—must be older even than that. No one knows how it
came there. It is composed entirely of those pale tints
which belong to the earliest form of colored glass, and
divided into two parts, one representing the Virgin with
saints, the other the death of John the Baptist, who has
the comfortable expression peculiar to most mediævally-
painted martyrs. The daughter of Herodias stands beside
him with her charger; in the distance is seen Herod at his
banquet.

The little church has another curiosity   Its silver
communion plate, flagon, paten, and chalice are inscribed,
"The gift of Madam Abigall Parnell to yᵉ Parish of
Antrim, A.D. 1701." And in the old register book is the
record, "Abigall Parnell, buried 1715." But the grave of
this excellent woman — for local tradition reports her to
have been really an excellent woman — is altogether lost.
No stone marks it, no one knows where it is. Could not
her "dear distant descendant," world-known now, spare a
few hours of his time, and a few pounds of his money, to
save from total oblivion the name of his paternal great-
grandmother, Abigall Parnell?

Had her burial been within the time of the present
sexton, she would not have been forgotten. "Sam" has
a wonderful memory. Out of his clear recollection of

every person he has buried for the last half-century, there
has been constructed a chart of the graveyard, so that no
new-comer of the defunct parishioners of Antrim can ever
interfere with another. Being congratulated on this by
the bishop of the diocese, Sam is reported to have answered,
"That he remembered his lordship's first sermon in that
church forty years ago.

"I told the text of it to my old woman. It was a very
fine sermon; and your lordship preached for two hours
and a half."

The good bishop (he is living still) turned away smiling,
and dived no more into the dangerous depths of Sam's pre-
ternatural memory.

As we left the church the day again clouded over,
though it was mild and pleasant still. We turned into Antrim Castle, Lord Massereene's, by the only entrance now
open, the stable gates; startling a collection of fowls and
children, who seemed masters of the melancholy spot—for
a dismantled, uninhabited house always looks melancholy.
Repairs were going on, and the pictures and furniture were
all swathed up, but we could see the fine proportions of the
old rooms, built in 1662, though the original castle must
have been standing in the thirteenth century. A "rath"
still exists in the gardens (for the Saxon readers I should
explain that raths are earthen mounds, into which the
ancient Irish used to drive their cattle, women, and children, for protection in war-time), showing that Antrim
dates from very ancient times.

The one curiosity of the castle is the Speaker's chair,

out of the old Irish Parliament.   At its last sitting, on the
10th of June, 1800, the speaker, the Right Honorable John
Foster, who had been violently opposed to the Union, took
the chair and mace away with him and refused to deliver
them up, declaring that he would keep both till they were
wanted for his successor, when there was again a parliament in College Green.   But he died without seeing this;
and his son, marrying the Viscountess Massereene, carried
off the treasures to Antrim Castle, "to be kept till called
for."   The mace we did not see, but of the chair I can
record that it is a very comfortable one to sit in.   Whether
its future tenant would find it so, if placed in a Dublin
Parliament, is an open question.

Dull and gray as the day was, my companions determined that I should not leave Antrim without having had
one sail—with oars and without sails, for that I insisted
on—upon the broad, calm bosom of Lough Neagh.   So we
secured a boat and man, and floated leisurely down the
Six-Mile Water, as it is called, a river, quiet as a duck-pond,
towards the lake.   Broad Lough Neagh was, but decidedly
not calm; in spite of old Peter and his two well-handled
oars, we felt as helpless among the big waves as if we
were dancing up and down in a cockle-shell.   Nor did
any sense of the poetical alleviate the discomfort of the
practical.

"Round towers, did ye say, ma'am?   Masther Moore"
(how did Peter ever hear of Masther Moore?) "wrote a
power o' nonsense about us fishermen, an' what we saw.
I knows the bottom of the lough, every yard of it, and

there's no round towers there, nor castles nayther; nothing
but fish, and mighty few o' them."

And then he opened up energetically on the subject of
fishing rights, or wrongs, of which he seemed to have a
good many; diverging afterwards to the question of eels,
and the best mode of killing them, which was equally
instructive. A curious mixture of Irish and Scotch was
this same Peter, keen and canny, though withal given to
"take it aisy," as, except when passion and prejudices are
concerned, is the way all over Ireland. He evidently
rather despised us for turning back, but we ourselves were
not sorry to exchange the big waves of Lough Neagh for
the placidity of Six-Mile Water, and the safe shelter of the
family hearth afterwards.

We had a cheerful evening, though sprinkled with much
political and religious talk, which I must ignore here. Yet
in Irish social life, just now, it is impossible to ignore it.
The heart of the country is full to bursting; it *cannot* hold
its tongue.

In England all shades of opinion are mixed up whole-
somely together. The phlegmatic Saxon may differ from
his neighbor at the polling booth, or regret that he goes to
another church, perhaps no church at all; so much so that
he would not like the said neighbor to be intimate in his
family, or marry his daughter. But he meets him at din-
ner-parties, and in railway trains, and interchanges social
amenities with him without the slightest hesitation. He
does not think it necessary to knock a man down for
presuming to differ from himself as to the government of

their common country, or to condemn him to eternal perdi-
tion for wishing to enter heaven by another road than his
own. But in Ireland—alas! alas!

However, even there are some calm - minded, sweet-
natured Christian men of all parties, who dare to hold
the balance even, and cross the line of social demarca-
tion, which in most cases is drawn sharp as if made of
swords.

"I would not contradict Mr. Blank, for he means well,
and he does not like contradiction," said to me one of these,
when I had been listening—mentally engaged the while in
the interesting process of dividing truth from imagination
—to an energetic Orangeman who, apropos of the Belfast
troubles, had given me a long account of other riots long
ago, which I had never heard of. "But it is only fair to
explain to you that the Catholics, not the Protestants,
began these disturbances, and that afterwards, to my certain knowledge, several benevolent Catholic families joined
together to recompense the sufferers."

"And how do you, with your wide experience, judge
between Catholics and Protestants?"

He smiled—the large-hearted smile of a just and good
man. "I judge not at all, I merely act. I do my best for
everybody, without distinction of creed. As a rule I find
my Catholic neighbors quite as easy to live beside as the
Protestants. They often send for me when they are sick
or dying, and I always go. The priest and I are very good
friends—in matters of charity we often work into one another's hands. Why not?"

Why not, indeed! If it were oftener so, how much better for poor Ireland!

August 19th.—There is, I have noticed, a curious certainty underlying the proverbial uncertainty of the Irish
climate. A very bad day is not unfrequently followed by
a good one—a day so heavenly that you feel, if the world
always looked like this, you would scarcely wish for paradise. We had many such on our journey, but none love-
lier than this day, when again we thought of the voyage
to Little Ram's Island. But, alas, it was impossible. My
young companions would be waiting for me, ready to start
on the coast-road to-morrow. I ought to be at Larne to-
night, and even my practical host and kindly hostess confessed that once afloat on Lough Neagh, there was no
saying when we might be back again. No, I must not be
faithless—Ram's Island could not be done.

"But we will not waste this lovely day. Let us walk
over to Steeple and see the Round Tower there. Your
artist" (who had preceded me at Shanes Castle, and elsewhere) thought it exceedingly fine—indeed, it is considered
the most perfect Round Tower yet remaining in Ireland.
And possibly it gave the name to the estate in which it
stands, for it is supposed to have been used as a steeple or
belfry."

A pleasant walk took us to this fine specimen of these
mysterious towers, found all over Ireland, about which
there has been so much speculation; but of whose date of
building—and builders—nothing has ever been discovered.

Pre-Christian they must have been,
though afterwards used for Christian
purposes, as this one. A cross enclosed in a circle is cut in stone
over its doorway, and at the
top are the remains of a beam
placed across, upon which a
bell probably swung. Its ex-
quisite proportions—being over
fifty feet in circumference at

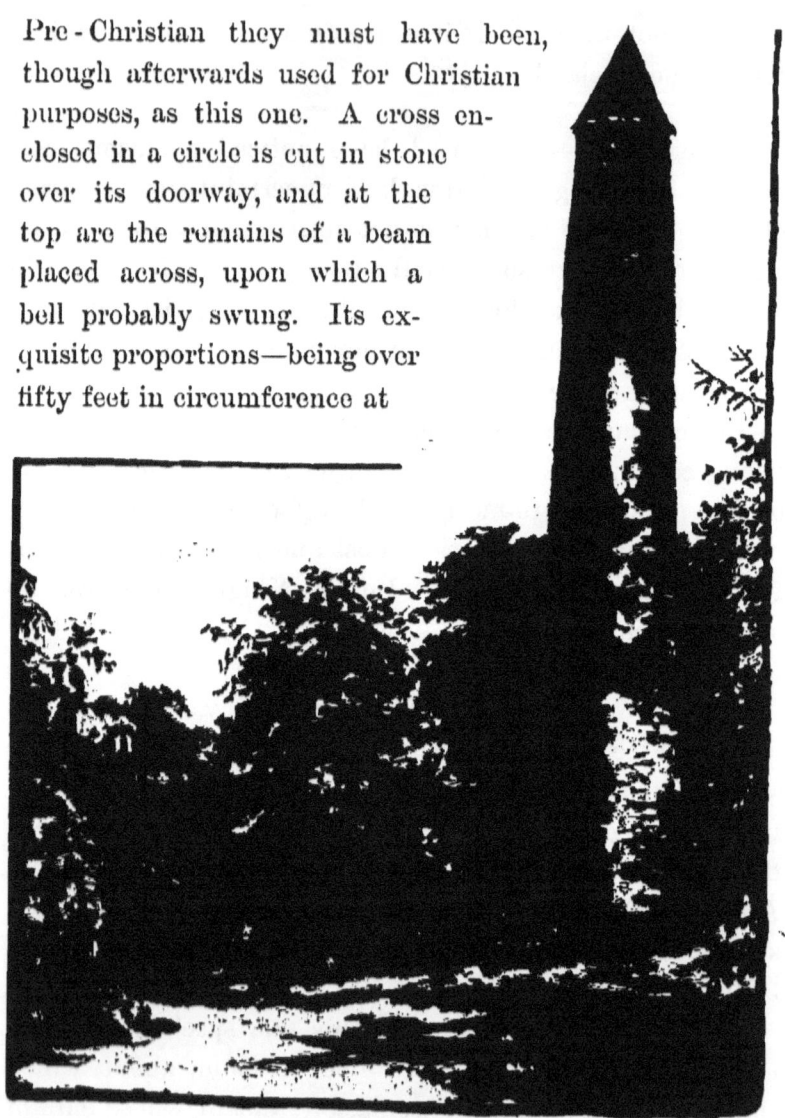

ROUND TOWER, ANTRIM.
(From a Drawing by F. NOEL PATON.*)*

the base and tapering gradually upwards — were very striking. Strange to see it in this pretty modern garden, and think of the hands that built it—the long-dead hands of an altogether vanished race.

"Yes, it's a fine tower, and it made such a splendid play-place for us boys," said the owner, who must have been a boy a good while ago. "It was struck by lightning in 1822, and had to be repaired. My father was always rather proud of it and careful over it, but we boys only thought of our play. We used to creep in at the doorway and look up to the top — ninety-three feet it is — where there are four slits of windows, east, west, north, and south, exact to the points of the compass. We thought it a pity so much good space should be lost, so one day we got a ladder inside, climbed up it, and laid planks across on the rough masonry, making a sort of loft. Then we planned another a little higher—I think there were three lofts in all—and we used to clamber up and down them. Oh! it was great fun!"

Very likely. Thus goes the world away. The handi-work of those unknown primeval people turned into a "splendid play-place" for the boys of the nineteenth century! Yet—what matters? Good work has always good uses—and finds a good end. So let the sun shine on this silent Round Tower, which keeps its secret with such a cheerful smile, and on the equally smiling garden below it, which must have been a burying-ground, for human remains were found when digging the flower-beds — which in their masses of gorgeous color were a delight to the

eyes. Thence we passed to the kitchen - garden — such a
garden! the first of many which I afterwards saw, and
which awoke in me the saddest sense of how Ireland
wastes her blessings—blessings of soil and climate equal,
or superior, to any European land.

While Irish cottage-gardens scarcely exist at all, the
gardens of "the gentry" are in many cases quite remarkable for fertility and beauty. Generally they are four-
square, protected by a solid stone wall from fifteen to
twenty feet high, with a little gate—alas, too often locked,
and they say, obliged to be locked, for poor, ignorant Paddy
cannot as yet be taught to see that the fruits of the earth,
like the fowls of the air, are not as much his as his master's. Within this sheltered space, flowers, fruit, and vegetables flourish altogether in wonderful luxuriance.

Oh, what a garden to possess! literally rampant with
plenty. Flower - borders on either side the neat gravel
walks; beyond these, long lines of gooseberry - bushes,
heavy with fruit, smooth or hairy, yellow, green, and red;
and espaliers laden with fast ripening apples and pears.
As for the raspberry-bushes, they were a perfect forest, six
or seven feet high—into which some one I blush to name
disappeared in the very middle of an interesting archæological argument, and was missing for several minutes! And
the vegetables, which, being kept in good order, were almost as pretty as flowers—it was a treat to see the gigantic old-fashioned artichokes, the rows of late pease and early scarlet-runners, and the dark - red leaves of the beet-
root contrasting with the bright green of the early kale.

"What a delight this garden must be! What a pleasure to turn into it a handful of holiday children — good children, who could be trusted not to eat themselves ill. How nice to walk round it with a big basket and think what one could send to friends who had no garden of their own—gifts that cost little to the donor, and are to the receiver a priceless boon."

They would be here certainly; for I was told that in Antrim, as in many a little country town, fruit and vegetables are almost unattainable.

"Nobody thinks of cultivating them — nobody knows how to do it. The cottager plants his bit of ground with potatoes, and, perhaps, a few beans—he never aims at anything beyond. As for growing vegetables or fruit to sell, such an idea never enters his mind. He would not do it even for himself, he would prefer to live on potatoes all the year round. Alas! in Ireland as elsewhere—but more in Ireland than elsewhere—the great difficulty is to get people to *take trouble*."

"But," I urged, "though revolutions generally come from below, reformations come from above. It is the upper classes who must educate the lower, and by practical aid and example rather than preaching. Suppose some enterprising horticulturist were to start a market-garden, he might do wonders with this fine climate and fertile soil, and by employing labor scatter among the poor money as well as instruction."

My companion shook his head sadly. "Utopian— Utopian! Your market-gardener might raise produce, but he would never sell it. And your laborer would never work. The Irish peasant has little notion of either luxury or comfort. Now, especially, he has lost all heart. His patience is wonderful, and so is his uncomplaining endurance. But he never tries to resist misfortune or avoid it. He would sit and let his cabin drop to pieces over his head before he would bestir himself to mend it."

The speaker was Irish, and had lived in Ireland nearly all his days. Alas! I found then, and often afterwards, that the most hopeless about the future of Ireland are the Irish themselves.

"But don't let us talk. Come and see the Witch's Stone—here—among the cucumber frames. *She* was an energetic Irishwoman — she leaped from the top of the

THE WITCH'S STONE.
(*From a Drawing by* F. NOEL PATON.)

Round Tower. You can see the mark of her elbow and knee where she alighted."

So we could. It was evidently one of those flat Druidical stones, supposed to be used for human sacrifices. The little circular holes, now filled with innocent rain - water, were made to receive the victim's blood. Surely we have gained a few steps in civilization since then. Life is held of more value, and made a little more pleasant and comfortable.

"Pleasant! comfortable! Our poorer classes hardly understand the words. They are half barbaric still. And yet there are in them certain qualities, mental and moral, which are altogether lacking in your English and Scotch peasant. And what the land is — how rich and plentiful it might be made, and is made, when the lords of the soil take trouble with it—you have but to look round on this garden and see."

So talked we—I will not vouch for the words, but I will for the substance — till we reached the friendly door which I was so soon to leave, and found waiting there a good-looking young fellow of nineteen or so—not exactly in rags, but very poorly clad. He had come to speak about his marriage! for the expenses of which his friends had subscribed five shillings.

"Yes; that is how we do it in Ireland," explained my friend. "And, perhaps, you may say it is the cause of our misery—and serve us right. But what is poor Paddy to do? The best part of his life is his youth. Our peasantry marry as mere boys and girls; but—they do marry; and they very seldom break the marriage-vow. Consequently they rear up a brood, wild and numerous as young pigs or chickens, but healthy and strong; the wholesome children of virtuous parents. On this point of strict morality, the pivot upon which society turns, there is not a country in Europe—statistics prove it—which can compare with Ireland."

A few hours more and I had left Antrim behind me, with all its pleasant recollections, and was safely landed at Larne—there to pick up my young flock and continue my journey.

August 20th.—One of the reasons often given against travelling in Ireland is that there are no hotels fit for tourists who have any sense of cleanliness or comfort; which was true enough some years ago, but is not now. For the encouragement of those who wish to see the wondrous beauties of this almost unknown country, I shall set down those places where the weary traveller need not fear to lay his head, as I did mine, and woke up to the loveliest morning and an unimpeachable breakfast, at the Older-fleet Hotel, Larne.

To feel "fresh as a lark"—though pretty well on in years and of limited physical capacities—one requires to have slept in a good bed, with quiet surroundings. All these are attainable at the Olderfleet, which was built near the site of an old castle by the late Mr. James Chaine, to whom Larne owes its harbor, its steam communication with Stranraer, and much of its prosperity. He must have been a remarkable man, full of benevolence and of untiring

energy. The talk of the neighborhood attributes his pain-
fully sudden death to his exertions in organizing the reception and departure of the Prince and Princess of Wales.
Two days afterwards, his kindly hand, the last they
touched in leaving Ireland, lay still in death. Gossip—
too new to be tradition—declares that he left orders to be
buried in a sitting posture on a little hill, whence he could
overlook his beloved Larne Harbor. A strange fancy,
which recalls the burials of the old Norse heroes. But be
this as it may, the good Belfast merchant was a hero in
his way, and has left two sons who well may follow in
his steps.

His influence has greatly helped on civilization. In-
quiring how we could traverse the splendid coast-road
between Larne and the Giant's Causeway, we found that
an energetic Mr. MacNeill had organized a system of
tourist and private cars, with good horses, and capable,
steady drivers. No fear of driving over a pig, as I remember doing in the streets of Belfast about thirty years ago,
and being answered, as the creature ran limping away,
"Och, miss, sure an' we often do it. It doesn't hurt them."
As for our driver, he looked sober as a judge; an honest,
kindly young fellow, whom everybody knew. And his
vehicle was not an outside car, which the timorous English
mind expected, but a comfortable wagonet.

Merrily we started, I and my third young friend, and
picked up the other two stray lambs from their delightful
temporary fold, where they had been shown no end of
kindness. They had seen several curious things — an

3

ancient cromlech, near the landing-place of Larne; the Giant's Cradle; a rocking-stone, said still to rock when any criminal approaches it; the village of Glynn, with its ruined church, and other places; one always hears afterwards of so many things left unvisited. But the great thing is to see all one can, and enjoy all one can.

As we certainly did; driving along the splendid road, a triumph of engineering, with overhanging cliffs on the left, and on our right the open sea, as blue and bright as the Mediterranean. Indeed, for many things, the road along the Riviera, which we go so far to see, is scarcely finer than this one, at our very doors. It wandered in and out, sometimes skirting tiny bays, sometimes cut through solid limestone rock, which is left in arches, but always carried high above the level of the sea, which in winter rages so furiously that the Two Maidens, lighthouses nine miles off, are for weeks shut out from all communication with the mainland.

But now the water lay still as a lake, and one could easily trace the opposite coast of Scotland; whence came invaders, harrying all the land, driving the native Irish into inland bogs, and colonizing the sea-board with a population who remain half Scottish, both in names and national characteristics, to this day, along all the Antrim shore.

What a lovely shore it was! Its beauties kept changing minute by minute. There were the Corn-sacks of Ballygally Head, basaltic pillars, of a formation similar to the Giant's Causeway; the detached rock on which are the few remains of Cairns Castle, and many another huge

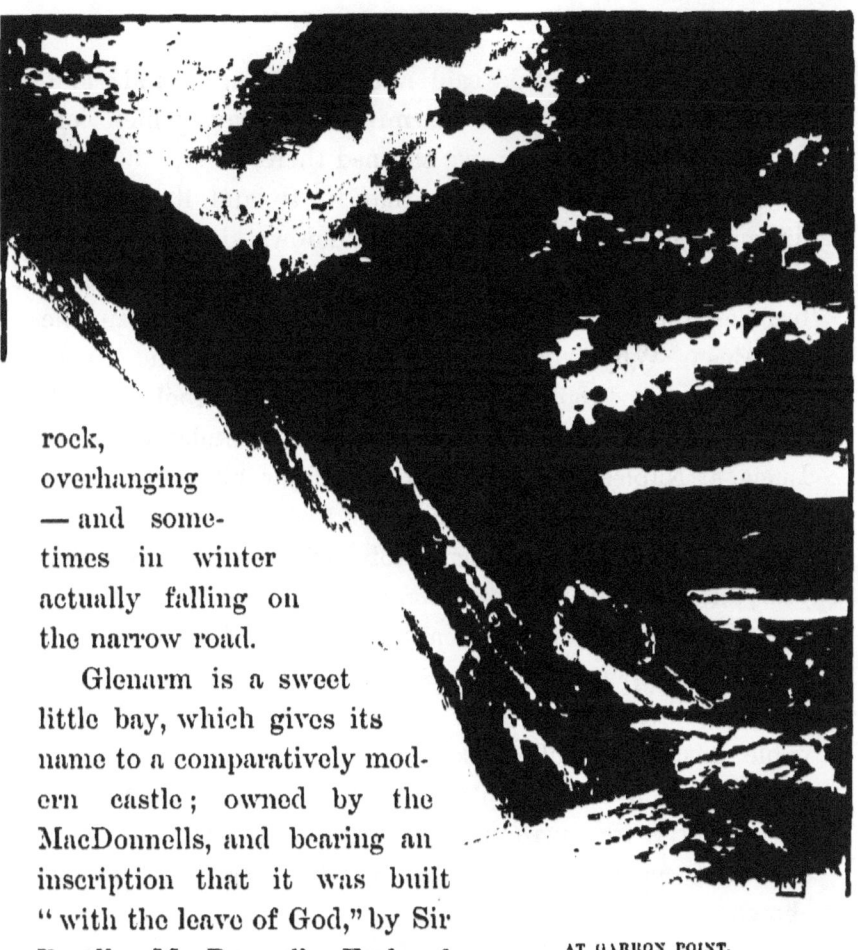

rock,
overhanging
— and some-
times in winter
actually falling on
the narrow road.

Glenarm is a sweet
little bay, which gives its
name to a comparatively modern castle; owned by the
MacDonnells, and bearing an
inscription that it was built
"with the leave of God," by Sir
Randle MacDonnell, Earl of
Antrim, "having to his wife
Dame Aellis O'Neill," in 1636. Excursionists often come
from Belfast for a pleasant day there, but we were obliged
to pass on, being due at Cushendall that afternoon.

"Your half-way house is Carnlough, where you can

AT GARRON POINT.
(*From a Drawing by* F. Noel Paton.)

lunch; we always did," said a too-confiding friend; and, lured by another of these charming little bays which continually indent the coast, we stopped there.

To our cost. Why is it that in Ireland it seems so difficult, next to impossible, that windows should be made to open, and doors to shut? that soap and water, brooms, brushes, and scouring-flannel should be almost unattainable luxuries? Why, when in despair we went out and "wandered by the brook-side," a really pretty brook, travelling seawards, should we find ourselves reminded of Santa Lucia, at Naples, than which, to those who know the place, no prettier word has an uglier sound?

I hear that the Carnlough Hotel will change hands this year, and so shall hold my tongue about it, except earnestly to advise the in-coming tenant to spend a few pounds in paint and paper, and a few shillings more in brooms and brushes, which, with one or two decent servants and a capable mistress, would make this little inn a most pleasant permanent halting-place on the beautiful coast road. How pretty its surroundings are, our artist, who went ahead of us, and suffered as we did, here has plainly shown.

Garron Point, a few miles farther on, was a delight to our eyes; and we longed to climb up the winding road at the left to Garron Tower, a small castle belonging to the Marquis of Londonderry, planted on a table-land, with the sea below and the hills above. Its gardens and grounds are said to be very fine, and its sea-views magnificent. But we had no time to stay and examine it, though this is

easily done
by getting an ad-
mission at the estate
office, Carnlough. We
felt we must hurry on. For
the bright day was clouding over,
and we had still a good many
miles before us.

COTTAGES NEAR GARRON TOWER,
(From a Drawing by F. Noel Paton.)

Headland after headland appeared and disappeared; the
sea turned gray instead of blue; the road seemed to wind
in and out in ceaseless curves. Curiously-shaped rocks,
with still odder names—one I remember, called the Spin-
ning-woman, and very like a sitting woman it was—were
pointed out from time to time. Also, we kept looking out
for certain picturesque cottages which had caught our
artist's fancy, and which are here depicted, and for a small

railway and quay made for some iron mines up one of these Antrim glens, now dilapidated and apparently disused.

"And there is Margery Bisset's castle," cried one of us, who had been here before, and who claimed to be a descendant of the said Margery Bisset. Concerning whom we put numerous questions to several people hereabouts, but could learn nothing about that respectable lady except the little heap of tumbledown walls which bear her name.

On, on, for we were growing tired, and beginning to wonder how the beautiful coast-road would look from under umbrellas, when turning round one more of the picturesque headlands, we came in sight of a pretty little village sitting in the midst of greenery, in the curve of a semicircular bay.

"There it is! I remember it now!" cried the great-great-great-granddaughter of Dame Margery Bisset. And as we drove up to the prettiest of inns, a smiling hostess, standing at the door, bade us " welcome to Cushendall."

Since writing the above I have received the following communication from a lineal descendant of the aforesaid Marjory Bisset—or, rather, as he spells it, Marjory Bysset:

"You have cut off my revered and beloved ancestress from about three hundred years of honorable antiquity. She was the daughter and only child of a Norman baron, who by hook or by crook had got hold of a large estate in the county Antrim. She married the founder of my

family, of the clan Macdonald, about A.D. 1390. Her son,
Donald Dhu, is the hero of Sir Walter Scott's spirited ode,
'Pibroch of Donald Dhu.' Being in command of the army
of the Lord of the Isles (chief of the clan), he gave a severe
defeat to James I. of Scotland, who, after Donald's troops
were disbanded, eagerly sought for him to behead him.
Donald fled out of King James's reach to his mother's
estate in Ireland, where he prevailed upon one of the
O'Neills to send to the king a head, presumed to be his—
upon which all pursuit of him was abandoned. To whom
the head belonged is not recorded, but it is certain that
Donald Dhu had no claim to it, for he was a noted leader
in the Highlands many years after King James's tragical
death.

"Marjory Bysset was contemporary with Richard II. of
England, who, in his two visits to Ireland, spent more time
there than all the kings and queens of Ireland from that
day to this, Victoria included. Without doubt the old
Norman baron presented his daughter at the English court,
where she became familiar with Richard's features and
appearance. After her marriage she must have been a
frequent guest at Ardtornish Castle, the residence of the
Lord of the Isles—a Macdonald, and either her father-in-law
or brother-in-law. You know that Shakespeare murders
Richard II. at Pomfret Castle; but contemporary Scottish
historians deny this, and say that the king afterwards
presented himself at Ardtornish, and lived for many years
at Stirling. Hill-Burton, in his lately published and valuable history of Scotland, relates this, and adds that 'he

[Richard II.] was recognized at the court of the Lord of the Isles by an Irish lady of the family of Bysset.'

"My family was driven out of Scotland in the beginning of the seventeenth century by James I. of England—with the aid of the Campbells. Our expulsion was attended with circumstances of extreme atrocity; which, but for accident, would have resulted in a massacre throwing the massacre of Glencoe completely in the shade. But for the secure refuge provided for us in county Antrim by the ever-blessed Marjory Bysset of Glenarm, our family would have become extinct."

The family—changed from Macdonalds into Macdonnells — have largely populated county Antrim. This clear and graphic account of their beginnings acquires additional interest from the fact that the writer is a gentleman who has just completed his ninety-first year.

PART II.

WE let the rain rain itself out all night without complaining. What was the good of complaining—especially in Ireland? Like wise travellers, we had provided against the possibility, nay, certainty, of being stranded for hours, or even days, in a solitary inn with nothing to do. We had taken with us books and work, and, above all, cheerful minds. So though the morning rose dull and mild, not actually wet, but very depressing, we refused to be depressed, and rejoiced in the near neighborhood of friends and the quiet shelter of the Glens-of-Antrim Hotel.

Though called "hotel" it is just a simple village inn; nothing grand or showy about it. But it sufficed for all our needs; we were thoroughly comfortable. We had good beds, good food, punctuality, cleanliness, and order; as well as that personal interest which is always so welcome in the inevitable homelessness of travelling. None of us can count upon being always well, always independent of kindliness, and to be ill, or to die, not in "the worst inn's

worst room," but in the grandest apartment of the best
hotel, would be a dreary thing.   If in our travelling we had
"come to grief," we felt we might have fallen into worse
hands than those of our good landlady at Cushendall.

The "we" here ought to be individualized and named.
To avoid personalities let me do it *lucus a non lucendo*,
describing each one of our party by a quality which she
does not possess.   For instance, the Bird, or the Brown
Bird, as she is commonly called among us, has shown no
disposition for nest-building, and never sang a note in her
life.   Then the Violet—it is her Christian name, but she is
certainly *not*

> "by a mossy stone
> Half hidden from the eye,"

being a hard worker in her college, and devoted to the
Higher Education of Women.   Thirdly, there was the
Wild Irish Girl, who is quite tame, and practical, though
full of fun, and brimming over with the brightness and
cleverness of her nation.

With these three girls — very different in their characteristics, but all sweet-tempered, sensible, merry, and har-
monious—one could have travelled to the North Pole, or
through the Desert of Sahara, and still found them satisfactory and ready to put up with everything—especially
myself.   The tenderest and most graceful thing I can say
of them is that they never once made me feel, as is sometimes done quite innocently and unconsciously, that the
old are a burden to the young.

If English invalids only knew it, there are along the

west coast of Scotland and east coast of Ireland—between which runs the warm Gulf Stream—sheltered nooks, where the climate is, all winter long, as mild as in Devon and the Isle of Wight. Cushendall is one of them. You may tell this by the sort of plants which flourish in its gardens, huge hedges of fuchsia, tall hydrangeas, and other shrubs, which in most parts of England die down to their roots every winter. Had this "prettiest village in Ireland," as it is called, been located farther south, it would soon have become a fashionable health-resort, full of genteel villas, streets of lodging - houses, splendid hotels, and every sort and kind of elegant frivolity.

Now, it lies almost unvisited, sweet and still, embosomed among its numerous trees and sheltered by the two arms of its beautiful bay. Only a few tourists pass through it, and some neighboring families come down in summer-time to disport themselves on the bit of smooth sand dotted with two or three private bathing-houses, to one of which my three young mermaids eagerly repaired, anxious to improve the time while waiting for the weather to clear up.

"You must go up some of the glens of Antrim," said one of the residents of the place, who had taken us in charge—as, indeed, they all did with never-ending kindliness. "These glens extend inland from the Antrim coast, like the fingers of a hand. Some are cultivated, others just bog and moorland, but all are different, and some most beautiful. You must go, if possible."

And she made it possible by the loan of horse, car, and man, with whom we afterwards went through so much, both of pleasure and—well, I will not say pain, though we had our difficulties—that to the end of our days I think we shall all remember Malcolm and his horse Charlie.

They stood at the inn door—in spite of a slight drizzle —ready to take us to the ancient graveyard of Layde, said to be the burial-place of Ossian.

"But, like King Arthur's in Cornwall, there are at least half a dozen graves of Ossian extant. Perhaps he was not buried in any of them. Very likely he never lived at all."

"Nor, possibly, did Homer, or Shakespeare. At least, Shakespeare may have lived, but some people say he didn't write his own plays. So you need not believe in Ossian, or waste time in searching for his grave."

So jested these young iconoclasts; but meanwhile we entered the old burying-ground, a curious place, situated near the shore, so near as to be scarcely fifty yards above high-water mark. The tide kept running in and out with a continuous murmur, and yet, as is the case all along this and the opposite coast, vegetation was green and luxuriant down to the water's edge.

"Come in," said our Wild Irish Girl, opening the little wicket gate. She had a sort of right to the place, as many of her forefathers repose there.

How desolate it looked! all the more so for a white goat tethered among the graves, and a man sitting upon one tombstone cutting letters on another. He was so absorbed that I spoke to him twice before he answered.

" Sure, ma'am, this is Layde burying-ground, and that's
the church ye see "—a few tumble-down walls, made into a
sort of open-air catacomb with iron railings. " How old
is it, did ye want to know ? There is a date somewhere.
I'll go and look."

Leaving his work, he went with us over the long grass,
and uneven ground, billowed with many nameless graves,
and pointed out a stone in the wall inscribed " Dinnis *(sic)*
McAulay, 1696."

" But the church must be a deal older than that ?"

" Maybe, ma'am. Nobody knows."

And apparently nobody cared, for the tombstones were
broken and dilapidated, the chapel a mere ruin. So was
a mass of masonry near the gate, which we were told was
called the Nun's Tower.

" There is supposed to have been a nunnery here once,
but nothing is really known about it," said the friend who
had brought us hither, and who went searching about for
her ancestors' graves amid the nettles and brambles. How
much these old heroes thought of themselves once! how
little anybody thinks of them now!

On either side the railings of the unroofed chamber of
graves, two tall stone tablets, like the Ten Commandments
over a church altar, pedigrees rather than epitaphs, com-
memorated two families, one being " Major Alexander
McAulay, from Ardincaple, Dumbartonshire," who was
" in the Scotch army of Charles the First in Ulster," and
who " married Alice Stewart of Ballintoy."

" Ballintoy is a village between here and the Causeway.

Probably Mistress Alice was one of the Irish heiresses whom so many enterprising Scotsmen came over and married."

"Or fought with them first and married them afterwards, as was the fashion then," said our Wild Irish Girl. "Here is another; Alister McDonnell. That must be he who was 'out' with Montrose; I ought to clear the nettles away from his grave, at any rate."

And as we stood round it a young thrush flew out of the mass of huge primrose leaves which showed what heaps of flowers there must have been among the graves last spring. It made us all start, yet seemed a bit of life—happy young life—in the midst of so much death.

"The birds often build in this tree, ma'am," and our civil stone-cutter pointed to a flourishing plane-tree that grew in the middle of the roofless chapel. "I knew an old man who saw it planted. He was a slip of a boy then, watching a funeral here, and he saw one of the bearers take a pole that the coffin had been carried with, and stick it into the ground to save himself the trouble of carrying it home. It took root and grew. Ye see it's a fine big tree now."

Our Wild Irish Girl corroborated this curious story; adding that she knew a lady whose uncle and aunt had been married under this self-same tree.

"Once a church always a church, so it was all right. But don't you think this would be a dull place to be married at?" In which sentiment all agreed.

To these young creatures marriage seemed a much

nearer and more interesting thing than burying. But I could not help thinking of the dead McDonnells and McAulays, and all their generations of long-closed graves —men and women, whose joys and sorrows, alike unrecorded, were so vivid and real once. Yet

> "They fly, forgotten, as a dream
> Dies at the opening day."

Happy those who, as they advance nearer to that earthly oblivion, can lift their eyes and behold still shining, somewhere, another " opening Day."

Malcolm never could have driven a merrier party than that which started this afternoon to visit two of the Antrim glens, going up Glen An and down Glen Dun. It was our English girls' initiation into the mysteries of an Irish car, which to the Saxon mind has but one advantage —you are always ready to jump out. At first they were so exercised in "holding on," greatly to the amusement of the Irish girl, that we hardly noticed the scenery for laughing. But when we began to mount, almost at a foot's pace, mile after mile, and the desolate glen opened out—all the grander for the dull, gray sky, with its constant threatening of rain, and all the more lonely for the "few sheep in the wilderness" that appeared now and again, staring at us with the usual silly, dazed look, and then scampering away —we were forced to acknowledge that there might be fine gloomy landscapes even out of Scotland.

At the high point, just where Glen An meets Glen Dun, we found a shooting - lodge, the first dwelling-house we had come to, and one of the very ugliest I ever beheld.

"What an idea the Irish must have of domestic architecture!" said the Brown Bird, who likes to have things pretty about her, and is rather critically minded.

"And what a ' dead-alive' place this must be to live in!" observed the Violet, who thinks it no advantage to be "half-hidden from the eye" of intellectual society.

"The gentleman that owns the place doesn't live here, he only comes for the shooting," Malcolm told us.

So all the rest of the year the beautiful stream runs brawling down, and the wide slopes of heather blossom and fade, innocent of tourists, who throng in crowds to much inferior scenery. But then, as I have said, this is an unknown country, and will be for generations, unless travellers from other countries should find it out and rouse it from its melancholy, hopeless condition of sloth and decay.

We had the glen all to ourselves; I think we had seen but two human beings till now. Then came a change. Instead of barren moorland we found patches of potatoes, even cabbages, while here and there a field of yet green oats, interspersed with masses of the pretty, yellow daisy which in Scotland is called "gules," showed a praiseworthy attempt at farming. The earthen banks, or rough stone dykes, which form the usual boundaries in Ireland, when there are any boundaries at all, began to be replaced by green hedges, adorned with quantities of honeysuckle, the largest honeysuckle flowers I ever saw. Evidently the land had good capabilities, even though it was only about two miles from the sea-board.

By and by we saw a village—at least two or three cottages which Malcolm dignified by that name. An old woman came out of one of them, whom he questioned as to where we should find " th' ould altar."

We had never heard of it; so he informed us that it was a very curious old altar in a wood, where the priest used to say mass until the last few years, when a gentleman, "an' a Protestant gentleman too, ladies," felt so sorry for the poor folks, kneeling out in the open air in all weathers, that he built them a chapel close by.

" An' a beautiful new chapel it is—and ye must go and see it. But maybe ye'd like to see the ould altar too," which Malcolm evidently thought a vastly inferior thing.

We thought differently. It was a most interesting relic of antiquity—prehistoric, evidently, for we could get no information whatever about its origin, till a young inhabitant of the glens, whom we afterwards met, volunteered to give me a written account of it. She has done this so well that I prefer her words to my own.

" Up Glen Dun, more than a mile from the sea, is an old stone altar, where the people used to worship long before there was any chapel in the glens. I don't know—nor does any one—how old the altar is. It lies in the hollow of a hill, outside Craiga Wood—the oak-tree being older than the altar, and the Runic stone older than the oak. Great stones form the back of the altar, which is supported by the roots of the ancient oak split in two, in

4

the clefts of which grow foxgloves and ferns. You can see where the old trunk was cut through, but two young trees have sprung from it, one on each side; their branches have spread and joined, making a close shade overhead.

"The altar beneath is in the form of all Christian altars, but with two arms built out on either side. In place of the crucifix is the Runic stone, as I have heard it called, though why I know not, for it seems to me like the broken top of an old Irish cross, or else has been shaped into a cross by whoever wished to Christianize it. The figure carved on it in deep relief, though much weather-worn, is either a Christ or a saint. It has outstretched arms—not straight, as when fixed on a cross, but one a little elevated above the other. Behind the head is an angel, with wings clearly discernible. Below are letters, but so much defaced that one cannot make out whether they are Roman or Irish characters.

"Connected with this altar, which, curious as it is, no archæologists have yet discovered or written about, is a superstition still firmly believed in. Tradition threatened any one who should hurt the tree or move a stone from the altar with a heavy curse. Some generations ago, a McAulay of Glenville, the richest man in all the seven glens of Antrim, dared to cut down the sacred oak — but, in spite of this, it did not die. The two branches it put forth have slowly grown together and formed a second tree, else, the people say, there would have been an end of the McAulays."

However, continual misfortune has followed the family,

which has lost nearly all its wealth, and for three generations there has only been one heir to the name—as there
is now. The present McAulay is a young boy in his teens.
I accidentally saw his photograph — a sweet, good face.
May the sacred oak and he live and flourish together!

We found Malcolm and his Charlie waiting outside the
new chapel, which he seemed so determined we should
admire. He was himself a good Catholic, though he told
me he had served from a boy, and his father before him,
the excellent Protestant family who had evidently won his
entire devotion. Partly to please him, we were going into
the brand-new modern building, when we were confronted
by a lovely apparition in the shape of a young girl on a
chestnut mare. She with difficulty reined in the pretty
creature, while she stooped to shake hands with our Wild
Irish Girl, who was delighted to see her. What a beaming
face it was! Involuntarily I thought of Moore's lines to
his Irish Girl:

> " For whilst I've thee before me,
>   With heart so warm and eyes so bright,
>   No cloud can linger o'er me—
>   That smile turns them all to light."

"So you have been looking at the old altar? Did you
see the well which some young priest once blessed? He
was dying, and his mother told him he ought not to die
without leaving some good thing behind him. So he dug a
hole in the moss with his hands, and blessed it, and it's a
holy well to this day."

(N.B.—I fear it isn't, for my girls afterwards sought for

it all over the spot which Malcolm pointed out to them, and found not a drop of water nor the ghost of a well.)

"And the fairies' thorn?" continued our eager young horsewoman. "Have you seen that? It's true — quite true. The thorn-tree was so old that it had never been known to flower—when, two years ago, it suddenly took to blossoming, and was covered with may. But being known as the fairies' tree, nobody dared to touch it. Some rash hands plucked a flower or two, and had heavy losses directly. I myself took some sceptical friends to see it— they would insist on gathering the blossoms—and do you know," with a curious mixture of fun and earnest in her lovely Irish eyes, "every one of them lost something!"

We all laughed. Though I did not say so, I could not help thinking that anybody going anywhere with that charming girl would be not unlikely to lose—something!

She told us all about the Catholic chapel. "Yes, is it not a pretty one? And it was really built by a Protestant. We don't hate one another in these innocent glens as you do in your big towns. When we had our bazaar for building a new church at Cushendall, the Catholics helped us a great deal. And as you will see, in this churchyard Catholics and Protestants lie side by side. Nobody objects."

"They did object in the old burying-ground at Layde," said our Wild Irish Girl. "My great-great-grandmother was buried a good many yards distant from the family grave, because she was a Protestant."

"It is not so here," continued the mistress of the chestnut mare; with difficulty—as the beautiful animal evidently disapproved of conversation. "There is one grave you must look at. A girl here who had second sight—as they call it in Scotland—begged her sweetheart, a fisher-lad, not to go to sea on a certain day, as he would certainly be drowned. He was drowned, though they managed to rescue his body and bury it in this place. The girl would sit for hours beside the grave, carving a ship on the stone, till at last she went melancholy mad, and jumped from a rock into the sea at Cushendun. Good-bye, till tea-time."

And she galloped off, while we crossed the—for once—carefully kept graveyard to the stone she indicated, and, pulling the moss away, read the inscription: "*Alister's burying-place. Here lies the boddy (sic) of John, his son. Died March,* 1803. *Aged* 18." Underneath, rudely scratched as with a nail or pin, was the outline of a ship, with the words: "*Your ship, love, is moored, head and stern, for—*" Here followed some Gaelic words, which we were told meant "forever with God." There were a few more half-obliterated marks, supposed to represent an anchor and a goat.*

My girls looked grave for two minutes or so, then we left, and all began laughing again. Life—young, happy life—put aside the idea of death. Besides, the gray, dull afternoon was brightening into a lovely evening, and Charlie started off, careering at a speed which made the science of "holding on"—to people not used to Irish cars—a very essential study. By the time we reached Cush-

---

* I have since heard that these marks were scratched, not by a love-lorn girl, but by the boy's father. My readers may choose either tradition.

endun we were all ready for a quiet saunter round another of those delightful walled-in gardens, full of flowers and fruit—and a hospitable tea afterwards.

Cushendun—the twin - village of Cushendall—is, if less pretty, decidedly the fresher of the two, being more on the open sea. The opposite coast of Scotland, that is, the Mull of Cantire, and I fancied the hilly outline of the dear familiar Island of Arran, were dimly visible. But just now my young folks found an attraction nearer home.

Three months or so before there had been a wreck of an emigrant ship, the *Lake Champlain*, off Cushendun. Her captain, stopping to put on shore some stowaways, had run her on the rocks, where she had ever since remained. An enterprising Belfast firm had bought her, just as she was, "for an old song," and risked the experiment of getting her off. For weeks workmen had been employed about her, inhabiting a large hut on the beach, and working, whenever weather allowed, with the help of a number of tugs, to get her afloat again; to the great interest of all the village, indeed, all the country-side.

"You must come and look at her," said a son of the house. "She lies just where she went ashore, close here. Every day they expect to move her, but still she sticks fast. No—by Jove, she's off!"

The energetic youth threw down the glass through which he was looking, and bounded over the wire fence like a shot. All the other young people followed. The Bird flew as if she had really wings; the Violet took to

her heels light as air. Even the Wild Irish Girl refused
to linger tamely behind, but rose up and fled after the rest.
We two elders were left alone.

"Well, you and I can't leap fences and clamber over
rocks, so let us walk quietly down to the shore and see the
Lake Champlain glide past."

So she did, tugged by two vessels, and followed by
several more. We could see her decks, full of moving
black dots, and her portholes, out of which poured four
continuous streams of water, showing how hard her pumps
must be working.

"But if they can only keep her afloat till she gets to
Belfast, the firm will repay themselves over and over again
for the sum they spent upon her. They were plucky fellows to risk it."

Pluck with perseverance added always rouses sympathy. It was pleasant to see a body of workmen and
villagers running eagerly to the shore, whence, as she
passed, they gave the rescued vessel the loudest and heartiest cheer.

"We have not had such an excitement for years. I
hope it may be many a year before we have such another,
for wrecks are not common here. Sometimes the weather
is delightful till near Christmas — except for accidental
storms. See how they have beaten to pieces that ruin
opposite, which was once a castle."

Some one, who likes old castles better than modern
steamboats, pricked up her ears at this, and began to investigate eagerly a pile of ruins opposite the house.

"How delightful! to have an old castle at your very front door. How old is it? What do you know about it?"

"Nothing," answered the young horsewoman, who looked as pretty out of her riding-habit as in it, and had kindly left the young folks' company for that of the old —"nothing, except that it has a Banshee."

"A Banshee!"

"Of course, since the castle belonged to the McQuillans, a real old Irish family long extinct. The McDonnells and McAulays and the rest of us are quite too modern to keep a Banshee."

"You never heard her cry?"

"No; but our people say they have, sometimes in the winter storms. Do you believe in Banshees?"

I could not say "Yes," and I would not say "No." My young friend looked much delighted.

"I am so glad; for I believe in Banshees and leprachauns, and all sorts of things. And I know an old woman who is certain she once heard a Banshee cry. Would you like to hear the story?"

I asked her to write it down, with other "quite true" stories which she then told me, but I could not possibly remember. Here it is. Of course, I ask nobody to believe it, but it is curious how tenaciously such beliefs yet linger in Ireland.

"There is now living in Bristol a Mrs. Linahan, an old Irishwoman, who has not seen her own country for forty years. She is old, poor, bed-ridden, and suffering, but patient and cheerful beyond belief. Her strongest feeling is love for Ireland, and she likes talking to me because I am Irish. Many a time, sitting in her little, close room, above the noisy street, she has told me about Banshees and Phookas and fairies—especially the first. She declares solemnly she once heard the cry, or *caoine*, of a Banshee.

"'It was when I was a little, young child,' she told me, 'and knew nothing at all of Banshees or of death. One day my mother sent me to see afther my grandmother, the length of three miles from our house. All the road was deep in snow, and I went my lone—and didn't know the grandmother was dead, and my aunt gone to the village for help. So I got to the house, and I see her lying so still and quiet I thought she was sleepin'. When I called her and she wouldn't stir or spake, I thought I'd put snow on her face to wake her. I just stepped outside to get a handful, and came in, leaving the door open, and then I heard a far-away cry, so faint and yet so fearsome that I shook like a leaf in the wind. It got nearer and nearer, and then I heard a sound like clapping or wringing of hands, as they do in keening at a funeral. Twice it came, and then I slid down to the ground, and crept under the bed where my grandmother lay, and there I heard it for the third time, crying, "Ochone! Ochone!" at the very door. Then it suddenly stopped; I couldn't tell where it went, and I dared not lift up my head till the women came into the house. One o' them took me up and said, "It was the Banshee the child heard, for the woman that lies there was one of the real ould Irish families—she was an O'Grady, and that's the raison of it."'

"And then, seeing I was rather grave — though my family are of the humble, modern race, only two or three hundred years old, so we don't keep a Banshee—Mrs. Linahan went on to tell me, in her poetical south - country language, about catching a leprachaun.

"'Did you ever hear tell of a leprachaun, dear? He's a little ould man, as cute as a fox, and as hard to grip hould of. But if ye can catch him and keep him safe for a year and a day, he'll tell ye where the fairy gold is lyin', and ye'll be rich ever after. Well, there was a foolish man away in Connaught—they're mostly fools there, my dear— and he catched a leprachaun sleeping undher some white clover, and carried him home, and then he was bothered intirely where to keep him. So he put him in a wicker basket turned upside down, close by the fire, right forenenst where himself would be always sitting on his creepy. "Faix! that'll do for ye now," said he, and went to get his supper. But the leprachaun set up such a hullabaloo, "Let me out, let me out, let me go to me wife and me childher," and kept up the same day and night, till the poor man was nigh crazed, and went into a tantrum and turned up the wicker basket. "Musha! go 'long out of that," ses he, and the leprachaun was up and away out of the door.

"'But wait till I tell ye, dear, of another man I knowed myself, that catched a leprachaun. He was an Ulster man, and they knows the ways of the world better nor them o' Connaught. So he never heeded the leprachaun's crying, but just said, "Whist, ye cripple! be asy now, as asy as ye can," till the year and the day were out. And then the leprachaun cried out in his little small voice, "The north side o' the hill, undher the great big stone. Let me out, let me out." So the Ulster man let him out, and went to the north side of the hill, and what he found there nobody knew; but he grew a rich man, and got to the very top o' the tree.' "

As many Ulster men do, with or without fairy gold. Nothing strikes one more in going among these Antrim glens, and along the Antrim coast, than the vital difference of race there is in different parts of Ireland. These Ulster men, hardy, industrious, self-reliant, need only the influx of a little more money, a little more education, with kindly guidance into that civilization which education alone can give, to become a valuable integral part of the empire. The best Home Rule for Ireland — and she needs sorely some Home Rule — is to cultivate among her ignorant masses those qualities which would make her fit to govern herself, and so take her level place with England and Scotland in the one United Kingdom.

We found that our artist, travelling on ahead of us, had missed the two sights upon which Cushendun prides itself — a fine viaduct, too modern for artistic purposes, which spans Glen Dun river, and some sea-caves and natural arches, noticeable anywhere but on this magnificent coast, which abounds in such. The ancient altar is so little known that he had never even heard of it! Therefore Cushendun must go unillustrated : a happy hunting-ground for future painters, who would find in the glens of Antrim material for a whole summer's work.

August 22.—And yet summer here seemed still at its prime. What a Sunday it was! like an Italian day, cloudless from beginning to end. What a contrast in its solitary peace to Sunday fortnight, when I had been lured to go, rather unwillingly, to the Spurgeon Tabernacle—quitting it with every respect for the man who, by his earnestness, attracts all sorts of people and "compels them to come in"—but with a determination never to go again myself. One almost regretted leaving the solemn, wordless preaching of the everlasting sea, for the little church of Cushendall, which the good Catholics had helped the Protestants to build, in this "sleepy, simple parish," as the preacher called it in his sermon. A sermon which enthusiastically begged our contributions for some South African Mission. I could not help thinking that a better mission would be the civilization of the starving semi-heathens in many parts of Ireland.

But the angry spirit, which I confess always awakes in me after hearing missionary sermons, was soothed by an afternoon saunter on the shore, and a delightful cottage tea, which will be to my English girls a perpetual refutation of the creed that—except the gentry—all Irish folk are untidy and uncleanly. Also a visit to a private Cottage Hospital, where the descendant of I know not how many old heroes—land-rovers and sea-robbers—spends her peaceful days in doing all the good she can to the sick of the neighborhood.

And here the Violet, who had never in her life been inside a Catholic chapel, begged me to take her to one.

Why not? Good Christians can say their prayers anywhere, with any other Christians who are in real earnest.

Though the congregation consisted mostly of what we call the lower classes, their reverent behavior was unmistakable. Old women, with the usual bright-colored plaid shawl over their heads, parents with their children, and a number of young men who had been lounging outside, crept quietly in, knelt and said their beads. The gathering twilight, the simplicity and hush of the place, made it feel sacred, until the priest entered, and in English, marked with a strong Irish brogue, and so rapid that it was almost as unintelligible as Latin, pattered over a service entitled "the Rosary of Mary."

I often think, if that meek and holy woman, "the handmaid of the Lord," whom we Protestants do not revere half enough—could look down and hear herself thus misinterpreted, how she would shrink from her so - called worship! It made us sad to listen, sadder still to think of those others who listened in the simplest and sincerest faith. But in those things no man has a right to judge his brother. Enough if he keeps his own faith firm, his practice right, and his conscience clear.

Still, I think the Violet, like myself, felt relieved when we got out into the still, sweet, golden-tinted evening, the Holy Catholic Church of nature, which is open to all and satisfies all.

Since writing the above a correspondent, quite unknown to me has sent me a letter, the substance of which

I think it but fair and honest to transcribe. It expresses—as I have often had to argue with those who condemn their brethren of an opposite, or even a slightly different faith from their own—that what people are supposed to believe is often not at all what they do believe, and that they ought to be judged accordingly. Or, better far, not judged at all. The matter rests entirely between them, their conscience, and their God:

"May I venture, as a Catholic, or, if it please you better, a Roman Catholic, to ask you to hesitate in believing that those who love and practise the devotion of the Rosary need in so doing give you cause for sadness.

"We, in the Rosary, find a prayer which fits in with all moods, and which can be made the vehicle for the expression of all our wants. It is a form of prayer which is acceptable to the learned among us, while it is easy to the simple and those ignorant of book-learning. What is the Rosary? Not what it is represented to be by those who, like yourself, evidently do not understand its nature or its object.

"It is a meditation upon the principal events in the life of our Blessed Lord and of his Mother. In it we dwell upon the joys of his childhood and youth, the sorrows and pains of his passion, and the glorious events which followed. St. Dominic, in his time, saw the need of making people think more of the life of our Blessed Lord—and in those days when printing was unknown, and reading a rare accomplishment, he happily conceived this plan of the Rosary. It is a prayer which is loved by the greatest as well as the humblest minds. We find it a comfort in sickness : when eyes can no longer follow the words of a book, our thoughts can dwell on the life of our Lord, and our lips express the needs and desires of the moment by the 'Our Father' or the 'Hail, Mary.'

"And if the Rosary is associated with Our Blessed Lady, it is so because she is our Lord's mother. We Catholics find that just in proportion as we are devout to her, so are we faithful and fervent to our Lord and Saviour. The lives of all of us whom we call 'Saints' have proved this — St. Benedict, St. Dominic, St. Francis of Assisi, St. Charles Borromeo, St. Vincent de Paul, St. Francis de Sales, St. Thomas Aquinas, St. Anselm of England — all loved our Lady, because in their experience it drew them nearer to their Lord and God. . . .

"The enclosed paper upon the Rosary of Mary was written nearly forty years ago by Miss Augusta Drew, author of the 'Life of St. Catherine of Siena,' and many other religious books, and now for the last thirty years a nun at Stone in Staffordshire."

August 23.—This Monday morning we had settled to go up another of the beautiful Antrim glens. There are seven —Glen Arm, Glen Ariff, Glen Ballyemon, Glen An, Glen Dun, Glen Sheaske, and Glen McKearin. Each one has a different character, and all are as yet equally unknown to artist, geologist, and antiquary.

Glen Ariff, whither we were bound, is the largest of the seven, and has two rivers tumbling down it; we could hear their noise rising up through the mist which filled the valley, and hid a view which, we were told, included the opposite coast of Scotland. Just before we reached our goal, after nearly two hours of steady ascent, which did the utmost credit to Malcolm and his Charlie, the white fog cleared a little, and we saw both sides of the glen, green with pastures and thick with plantations, which it owes to the land-owner—Mr. Conway Dobbs.

The Dobbs family rivals the McDonnells and McAulays in the persistency with which it has taken root here, ever since the time of its first ancestor, Captain Dobbs, son of a city magnate in the reign of Edward VI. This branch of it owns a large estate; in fact, nearly the whole of the glen. Well planted, well cultivated, and dotted with thousands of sheep, the only blot on the beauty of Glen Ariff is the red patches caused by the working of iron mines, opened ten years ago, when a railway down to the sea was also made. Now, the price of iron ore having suddenly fallen, the works are stopped—the railway useless. But it will take a good while before Nature can repair the damage done her. Lord Antrim, who owns the mineral royalties of the glen, being an absentee landlord, does not suffer from this ugly invasion of the beautiful by the practical—but other people do.

A waterfall which our artist sketched, in defiance of a whole army of midges, is very beautiful. Near it—or near Cushendun (there are two traditions, each equally well attested)—the great Shane O'Neill, that proud chieftain who used to sign, "I am Shane O'Neill," is said to have been murdered by the McDonnells, whom he had defeated two

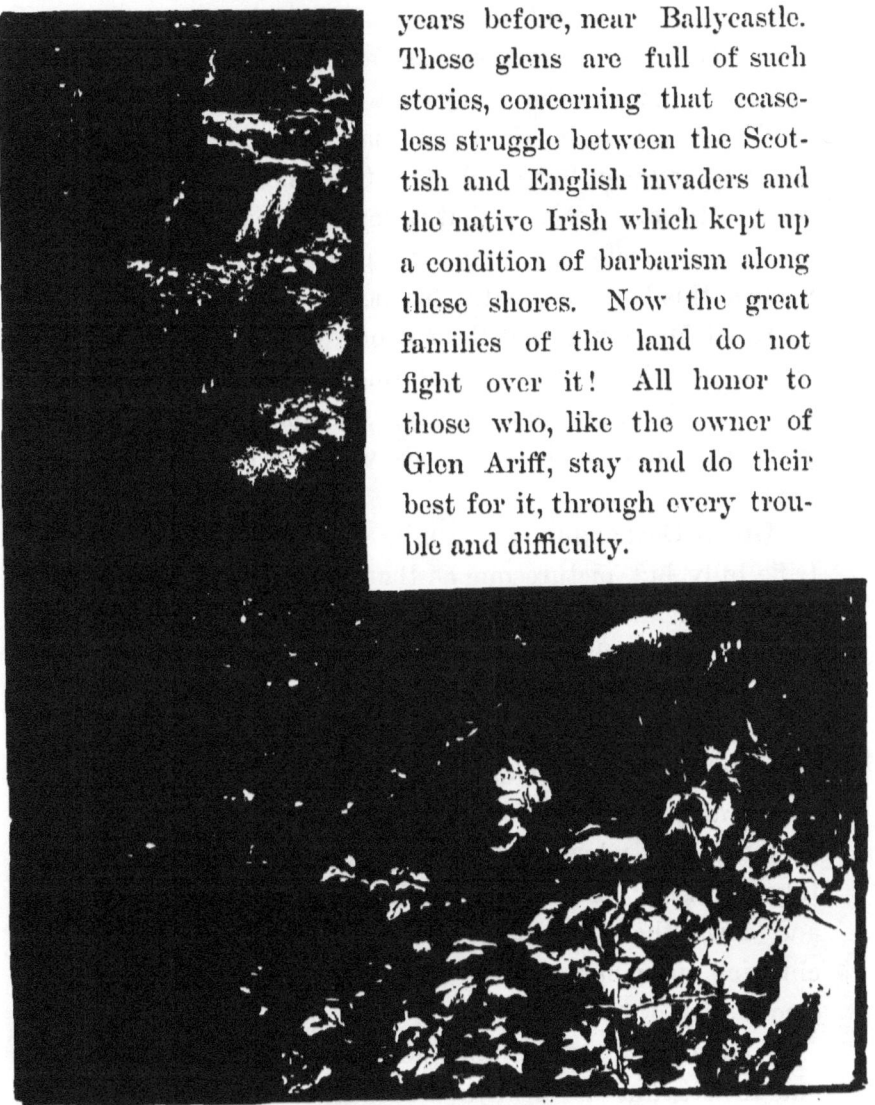

years before, near Ballycastle. These glens are full of such stories, concerning that ceaseless struggle between the Scottish and English invaders and the native Irish which kept up a condition of barbarism along these shores. Now the great families of the land do not fight over it! All honor to those who, like the owner of Glen Ariff, stay and do their best for it, through every trouble and difficulty.

WATERFALL AT GLEN ARIFF.
(From a Drawing by F. Noel Paton.)

August 24. — And the loveliest day that ever "came out of the sky." Also, our last at Cushendall. We were due at the Giant's Causeway that night.

"You *must* go by the coast road," said our friend. "It is a little rougher, but much finer than the ordinary tourist-road. Malcolm declares that if you will send your luggage on by a separate car along the good road, he can easily manage this bad one—with Charlie."

Good Malcolm's zeal, I fear, outran his discretion, but we assented ignorantly as gratefully, and started on an expedition which we shall always remember as one of the grandest — and roughest — roads we ever travelled in our lives!

Up to Cushendun, and a mile or two beyond, it was a trifle hilly, but picturesque as that which winds along the Mediterranean Riviera. And no Ansonian sea could be bluer or calmer than that which lay beneath us. As empty too—scarcely a boat or sail dotting its solitary breast.

The land was everywhere well cultivated, though so close to the sea. Fields of oats waved on every bit of comparatively level ground, potatoes flourished in nooks of the cliffs; where, built in any possible corner, nestled tidy cottages. Bright-eyed children, quantities of fowls, and cows that seemed to have the talent of goats for climbing anywhere, implied an industrious and thriving community.

"Ye're right, ma'am," said Malcolm, pausing to converse and to breathe—he always descended and led his horse, uphill and downhill, as we began to notice. "They're well

off, most of them farmers. They pays their rint, and the
masther's very kind to them." Evidently the fierce battle
between landlord and tenant was only a tumult heard afar
off on this fortunate coast.

Every minute it grew more beautiful—and more difficult. The girls were always getting out and in, and the car
itself took an inclined plane now and again, which made
" holding on " an anxious necessity. The intervals of level
ground became so few that all who could use their legs did
so. For Charlie—his tottering legs were painful to behold,
but his devoted Malcolm encouraged him—and me.

"Don't throuble yerself, ma'am. Charlie can do it. I'm
holding his collar up. It was just about this place that a
horse in a car with some gentlemen got choked with his
collar, going uphill, and dropped down dead on the spot."

After this cheerful information I tried to look as if
there was nothing on my mind, but while I kept one eye
on Tor Point, Fair Head, etc., etc., the other was fixed on
Charlie.

My girls walked on and on, it must have been for over
twelve miles, and declared this was the most splendid place
imaginable. The views changed every minute; the air was
so bracing that they felt capable of anything. I know not
whether we were glad or sorry to reach the bit of green,
high table-land where, it had been kindly arranged, a little
trap should meet us to take me down the very steep descent and up the ascent, at Merlough Bay.

It was not there. No sign of it, or of anything. Suddenly Malcolm remembered a painful fact.

"It's fair-day at Ballycastle, and there'll not be a man in the place—or a horse."

This was serious, as we had trusted to getting a car here—our luggage, on another, having preceded us to Bally-castle.

"Never you mind, ma'am," said Malcolm, cheerily. "If it comes to the worst we'll give Charlie an hour or two's rest, and I'll take yez on to Ballycastle. I'll get home by daylight to-morrow morning."

And then he proposed that the young ladies should descend to Merlough Bay, while he "tuk care o' the old lady"—which I must say he did most faithfully.

There was no road, but we jolted patiently across the moor, he leading Charlie, and I holding on as well as I could, till at last I begged to be allowed to walk, for a treat. At last we reached a farmhouse—whence, as Malcolm had foreseen, every available horse and man had vanished. He took possession of the empty stable, intro-ducing me to the house, and to the mistress's kindly hospitality.

She was certainly "well off." The furniture in her parlor—a beautiful old clock, and presses of mahogany, almost black with age—would have delighted a collector. There were pictures of saints, and white images of the Virgin and her Child. "We're all Catholics in these parts," Malcolm had said. And though the hens and their fami-lies ran about the floor, and more than one shepherd's dog rose up angrily from before the turf fire, where he lay with the children, the place was exceedingly tidy, and the basin of hot bread and milk which the mistress gave me was truly delicious. I say "gave me," for it was only by stealth that I was able to insert a small coin into the baby's pudgy hand. She would have given me tea, or anything else she had, with the heartiest hospitality.

Not less kindness did the girls meet with. Malcolm and I, sitting like two crows on the hilltop, and talking with that mixture of friendliness and entire respect peculiar to Irish servants, waited anxiously for them, and at last watched them slowly mount up from the bay—such a beautiful bay! ("But *you* couldn't have done it," said Malcolm, consolingly.) They had lost themselves, and got almost into despair, when they saw a farmhouse. The mistress took them into a most comfortable kitchen, where, in front of a large fire, upon a luxurious bed of straw, and surrounded by her eleven new-born babies, lay an enormous sow!

"The good woman seemed very proud of her interesting invalid. 'She's not a bit o' throuble, the crathur! Only she snores so I can't sleep o' nights.' It was the funniest sight we ever saw."

And my two English girls laughed at the recollection as if they never could stop laughing. They had been most hospitably treated, and offered hot potato-cakes—bread is rare in this region—but they were still able to attack the provision - basket which had been kindly filled at Cushendall. And they spoke enthusiastically of the beauty of Merlough Bay, which, alas, I could not behold. And then Charlie, reappearing as fresh as ever, and Malcolm cheerily

5*

declaring that the additional five miles of his journey were "no throuble at all at all," we were ashamed to feel tired, and started off boldly for Ballycastle.

"Fair Head in foul weather," as our artist saw it and has depicted it, we did not see, for it stood out clear against

FAIR HEAD IN FOUL WEATHER.
(*From a Drawing by* F. NORL PATON.)

the bluest skies, with the calmest of seas below. We longed to have been able to do—what all tourists should do —take a boat at Merlough Bay, and row under this grand headland, with its basaltic pillars, three hundred feet high, its other broken pillars lying on the beach below, and

above, the Gray Man's Path—another pillar which, in its
fall ages and ages ago, has lodged across a chasm in the
rock, and up which on stormy nights a gray man is said
to stalk. On the top of Fair Head are three fresh-water
lakes, in one of which may still be traced the remains of an
old lake dwelling, and not far off a cromlech once used for
badger-baiting. "The fine old Irish gentleman" of yesterday—perhaps even to-day—was more of a sportsman than
an archæologist. Bonamargy Abbey, which we passed a
short distance from the road
(it really was a road, level
and good at last!), would
never have had its ancient
ruins disfigured by a hideous,
slate - roofed, modern excres-
cence, and its tombs — it was
for four centuries the burial-
place of the McDonnells—broken, defaced, and destroyed.

TOMB OF THE FIRST LORD ANTRIM AT
BONAMARGY.

(*From a Drawing by* F. NOEL PATON.)

Ballycastle, which we
were now approaching, was a hundred years since a flourishing town. Its valuable coal-fields, extending along the
coast to Merlough Bay, belonged to a Colonel Boyd, whose
influence brought about the erection of a fine harbor. But
he died, and all fell into decay. The harbor became a ruin,
the docks a green field. Speculators worked the coal-fields
by fits and starts, but always at a loss, and Ballycastle was
fast sinking into oblivion when the railway between Belfast and Portrush stopped at it—and saved it.

Now, to all appearance, it is a thriving place. As we passed through its suburbs we noticed several good, nay, handsome houses. Its market-place was crammed with people. In addition to the groups of men and beasts that we had met coming from the fair, booths, with dancing and theatrical *artistes* outside, attracted each its little crowd, and in the midst I saw more than one woman trying to soothe or lead home a drunken husband — whom nobody minded, or only laughed at.

Such sights from the hotel windows did not encourage us to stay the night there, nor did a little episode in the coffee-room — which we shared with a gentleman and his wife. She lay on the sofa and looked as if she had been crying. Suddenly the window was thrown up from outside.

" Will your honor have the carriage round at six ?"

" At six," answered " his honor," rather grumpily.

" And will ye have the bull tied behind it ?"

" Certainly, certainly." At which we did not wonder that the lady on the top looked cross as well as tired. But it was evidently the custom of the country.

We thought, in case the bull might be going our way, we had better drive off at once; so we bade a cordial and grateful adieu to Malcolm, who persisted that he should be home " long before daylight," and that Charlie would not be a bit the worse. Then we departed, in a wagonet this time, where if we dropped asleep—not unlikely!—we should at least be safe from falling off.

The evening shadows, and a slight drizzle, made us less

eager after scenery, yet when our driver said, " Carrick-a-
rede, ladies," my girls roused themselves and insisted, under
the guidance of a small, a very small, boy, who was cap-
tured hard by, on going to see it. In their absence our
driver politely began to entertain me.

" I druv a young gentleman to Carrick-a-rede the other
day, who made a pictur of it. He was a fine young gentleman and well up to things. He seemed to think we were
all Home-Rulers, but I tould him no, the queen has as loyal
subjects in Ireland as she has anywhere, if she only knew
it. There's a gentleman named Parnell, as makes a great
talk, but half of us don't know him, or care for him. And
there's Mr. So-and-So, and So-and-So—"

Here he entered into a long political tirade, which I will
not repeat, and, indeed, can scarcely remember; except that
he wound up by wishing that it would please Providence
to take a certain old man—who had been, as I insisted, a
good and great man in his day—to another and a better
world. I only name this to show how fierce on both sides
are the political parties who tear Ireland to pieces between
them—as fierce as the feuds of those semi-savages who
fought with Shane O'Neill and with Sorley Boy M'Donnell
along these very shores.

Dunanynie Castle, where this renowned Sorley Boy was
born and died—quietly in his bed, for a wonder!—is the
merest ruin. But Dunseverick Castle, which now loomed
large in the twilight, and distracted my girls' attention
from the wonders of Carrick-a-rede (of which more by and
by)—is a much older fortress; indeed, it is said to have

DUNSEVERICK CASTLE.
(From a Drawing by F. Noel Paton.)

been built by a Milesian from Asia Minor in the year of the world 3668! Certainly it is mentioned in the "Annals of the Four Masters," as having been visited and blessed by St. Patrick.

We longed to stop and investigate it, standing on its detached island-rock, absolutely impregnable from the sea, and only connected with the mainland by a natural portcullis—a strip of green a few yards wide. But the gathering darkness would have made such an attempt very unsafe. And we had still before us miles of gloomy, unknown road ere we could reach the Giant's Causeway.

What it was like, or what sort of refuge we should find there for our weary bones, was equally unknown to us, but we were too worn out to speculate. I rather think for the last mile or two we sank into total silence; the road seemed interminable, and we felt as if it were years since we had left the happy shelter of Cushendall.

But every journey comes to an end some. time; and never did weary wayfarers hail a pleasanter sight than the gleam of light from the opening door, or enjoy a more welcome tea, and still more welcome bed, than we did when we arrived at last at the Giant's Causeway.

PART III.

THE GIANT'S CAUSEWAY.

EVERYBODY has heard of the Giant's Causeway, but it is strange how few out of Ireland, or even in Ireland, have seen it. Probably because it is considered—and perhaps was, till late years—a sort of Ultima Thule of civilization; its nearest links to which, Portrush, Port Stewart, and Bushmills, being, half a century ago, little more than villages. And any one who knows what an Irish village is now, can imagine what these were then.

Port Stewart afterwards grew into a small town, and was well abused as such by one young writer, who just passed through it—William Makepeace Thackeray—and as heartily praised by another—Charles Lever—who was for some time its dispensary doctor, and married there. Meanwhile Portrush became a railway terminus and a genteel watering-place. But little Bushmills remained *in statu quo*, innocent of tourists, bathers, and sight-seers; known only as the nearest point to the celebrated Giant's Causeway; until an enterprising engineer, Mr. W. A. Traill, conceived the idea of utilizing its river—the Bush—for the water-power of an electric railway; and so opening up the country, with all its wonders. These are, magnificent coast scenery; ruined castles, abbeys, and burial-grounds; cromlechs; Druidical circles; lake-dwellings, and underground caves—treasures dating from prehistoric times, and absolutely priceless to the artist and the archæologist.

But even these learned gentlemen must eat, drink, and sleep, and have a few more comforts than are supposed to be found in an Irish cabin, where the family repose, stretched out like the spokes of a wheel, with their feet towards the turf-fire—of which the smoke goes out by a hole in the roof. A slightly imaginative description of life in Ireland—which English tourists will not find realized anywhere; certainly not at the Causeway Hotel.

Arriving dead tired, we noted nothing except that we speedily got a most welcome tea—and a still more welcome bed. Awaking next morning, it was to find ourselves in a large, but not too large, hotel, planted on a rising ground near the sea. From the seven windows of its coffee-room and drawing-room one could trace the little bay below, the outline of shore beyond, and then away, away, across the wide Atlantic—our "next door neighbor," they told us, being New York. Malin Head, the last point at which transatlantic voyagers see land, was dimly visible in the distance.

But where—and what—was the Giant's Causeway? Of course we had read about it, and some of us had seen pictures of it; but I think even the Violet—the most learned among us—had very vague ideas about it. Should we attack it by land or by sea?

"By sea is best, and then you can row first to the caves, which are very fine," said a visitor who, in response to a letter of introduction, had appeared at nine that morning, and soon turned from a stranger into a friend. "I should advise you to start at once—it is a calm day" (alas! his notion of "a calm day" and ours, we found afterwards, did not quite coincide). "You may not get such weather again. How soon can you be ready? and I'll find you the best guide I can—John King—he knows everything, and everybody knows him."

Shortly John King stood at the door, cap in hand; a shrewd-looking, intelligent Irishman, elderly but not old, wiry and weatherbeaten.

"Sure, ladies, it's a beautiful day, and I've got ye a good boat—and I'll take yez down to the landing-stage in no time."

The landing-stage—our artist has sketched it—was a flat, smooth rock at the foot of a deep descent, down to one of the many small bays that indent the coast. We had the place all to ourselves, for the hotel was nearly empty—as it had been, we heard, from the time the Belfast riots began; and the little handful of tourists who come by rail and car for a "day out" rarely appear before noon.

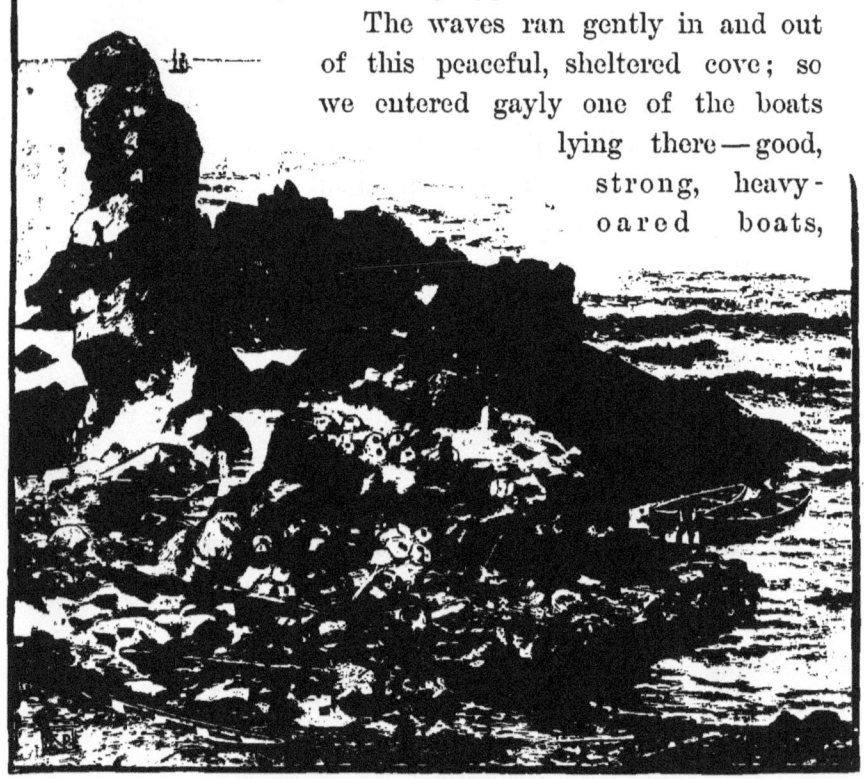

The waves ran gently in and out of this peaceful, sheltered cove; so we entered gayly one of the boats lying there — good, strong, heavy-oared boats,

LANDING-PLACE NEAR THE GIANT'S CAUSEWAY.
(From a Drawing by F. NOEL PATON.*)*

looking as if accustomed to be much knocked about by the waves. As in a few minutes more they certainly were.

I am no geologist, and when John King began to dilate on basalt and limestone, strata and formations, I felt exceed-

ingly small. So did the Brown Bird, and so also did the
Wild Irish Girl—in spite of her hitherto proud position
among the castles and graves of her forefathers. The Violet
alone was equal to the occasion. We left her to sustain conversation, and admired silently Portcoon Cave—where a her-
mit giant, who had vowed to eat no food from human hands,
was fed by seals, which brought it to him in their mouths;
and Dunkerry Cave, four hundred feet long by sixty feet
high, and only approachable by water—not habitable, therefore, even by giants. Its solemn black basalt walls, against
which great hillocks of waves slowly rose and fell, gave one
a strange sense of the power of the sea, and the utter pow-
erlessness of petty man.

By and by our heavy boat began to toss like a skiff on
the huge rollers that came tumbling in from the Atlantic.
And when the Bird quoted gravely a verse from some anonymous poem—

> "There's a sort of an up-and-down motion
> On the breast of the troublesome ocean,
> Which gives me a shadowy notion
> That I never was meant for the sea"—

we all coincided so heartily that John King's proposal to
"take the long course" and row round the Pleaskin was
decidedly negatived. I fear he despised us; but we were
content to be despised.

What he must have thought of our learning after his
experience with "Huxley and Tyndall," as he familiarly
called them, we dared not speculate. We only inquired

respectfully what these shining lights had talked about when they visited the Giant's Causeway.

" 'Deed, ma'am," said John, with a twinkle of his shrewd eye, " they didn't say much. Ye see, they wanted to get as much out of me as they could, and I wanted to get as much as I could out of them. Sure, them professors is much the same as everybody else, to my thinking. I tuk out the British Association some years ago. There were several boatfuls, an' I showed 'em everything, but they didn't say much. It was a middling fine day; though not so calm as this one."

Calm indeed! We did not contest the point; only hoped the British Association had enjoyed itself.

But now for one brief explanation, in the humble way in which alone I dare offer it, to readers possibly as ignorant of geology as myself.

For one thousand square miles on the north of Ireland there extends a sheet of basalt, varying from ten to a thousand feet in thickness. It is a sort of volcanic lava, which must have been poured out, molten, uncounted ages ago. To volcanic action is also ascribed the fact that when this sheet of basalt nears the coast it becomes columnar in character. Fair Head, Bengore, the Pleaskin, are promontories composed of enormous pillars, which at Port-na-Spania—a little bay so named because one of the Spanish Armada went to pieces there—slope gradually down to the sea, forming a perfect causeway, which may possibly extend right under the sea to the opposite coast of Scotland. On the islands of Staffa and Iona the same formation reappears, giving rise to

THE PLEASIN AND LIANS LA

the legend that it was made by Fin MacCoul, the Irish giant,
out of politeness to a Scotch giant, whom he wished to
come over and fight him, "without wetting the sole of his
foot."

John King told us this, and many other stories; pointing out the Chimney-tops, the Giant's Organ, the Giant's
Grandmother, etc.—Irish imagination gives a name to everything. And this opportune moment, when the boat was
pitching violently, the boatmen chose for showing us boxes
of specimens—which we devoutly wished at the bottom of
the sea. Hopeless of purchasers, they pulled up, and suddenly bade us land. The younger folk eagerly leaped out.
For me, when at my age you find yourself with one foot on
a slippery water-worn rock, and the other—nowhere particular, with the boat sinking from you into the trough of a
big wave, the sensation is—not exactly pleasant! I owe it
to John King's strong arm and steady hand that, instead
of sitting here writing, I am not at this moment quietly
sleeping among the two hundred and fifty Spaniards who
lie drowned in the little creek beside the Giant's Causeway.

Most people on first sight of the Causeway are disap-
pointed, but every minute's observation lessens this feeling.
It is a wonderful place—like nothing else in the world. Imagine a great sloping natural jetty, jutting out into the sea,
its floor composed of vertical basaltic columns, on the tops
of which you walk—the bottoms being sunk deep into the
sea. There are forty thousand of these columns, and they
are set so close together that they form a pavement; fitting
as neatly as a parquet floor. Hexagons, septagons, penta-

gons, are all as exact as if outlined by a human hand and a carpenter's rule. The columns are not formed of a single ·block, but in pieces varying from one to two feet high, piled each on each, and wedged firmly and fitted in together, the one end being convex and the other concave. Nature mimics Art so perfectly that it is difficult to believe the whole was not the handiwork of man.

In spite of our guide's voluminous and rather oppressive information as to details—such as the one triangular column, the three nine-sided columns, the Giant's Loom, and the Lady's Wishing-chair—whereon sat a respectable young person with a strong Belfast accent—the impression of the place was so mysterious and unaccountable that a sense of awe crept over us. What strange agencies must have been at work—what eons after eons must have slipped by since the making of the Causeway! There it is now, and will remain until the end of the world. Yet two hundred years ago it was absolutely unknown. There is no record of it in any ancient Irish literature; and in "Lord Antrim's Parlor" —a nook in the rocks, chosen by the omnipresent British tourist whereon to inscribe his all-important name—the earliest date cut is 1717.

The tradition of the Spanish Armada, which attempted to sail round this coast, and was wrecked there, vessel after vessel, is still rife. About the one lost at Port-na-Spania there is no doubt. The story runs that the captain mistook the three Chimney-tops—rocks exceedingly like chimneys— for the pinnacles of Dunluce Castle, and so ran ashore. Every soul perished, except four sailors who were picked up

alive. For centuries Spanish coins were occasionally found
on the beach at low water, and one large chest full of treasure was taken to Dunluce Castle. Thence, long after, it
was removed to Ballymagarry and Ballylough; being
finally claimed by the Earl of Antrim, in whose possession the empty coffer—the treasure having long vanished
—still remains.

John King, though he conscientiously pointed out the
spot and told the tale, seemed more interested in a modern
shipwreck—one of those tragic stories which must be common enough on this dangerous coast. An American liner,
the *Cambria*, had been wrecked in sight of land, and every
soul perished.

"She went down just over there" (by Malin Head).
"Some of us rowed out to her, but it was too late. We
brought home one dead woman in the bottom of the boat."

He spoke of it in a matter-of-fact way—as if an every-
day occurrence in these parts. But the awful element
with which they have to deal has its effect, moral and
physical, on a seaboard race. John King, though long over
sixty, looked hale and hearty, had an arm of iron, and
muscular, surefooted limbs that many a young man might
have envied. "I'm not done yet," he said, with a smile,
when he told me how old he was: and may it be long before he is "done"!

At parting he presented me with a four-leaved sham-
rock—that rare find which grants every wish of the possessor; offering another to the Violet—whom he seemed
to regard with greater respect than any of us. Doubtless

she will keep it and benefit by it. I gave mine away
where it will be more useful than to me, whose "wishing" days are all done.

Returning to lunch, we found the empty coffee-room
enlivened by a hot discussion between two new-comers—
a mild and rather melancholy-looking American and a
rotund specimen of "John Bull"—the John Bull who has
made himself (or rather his money, a very different thing),
and considers all the world, except England, scarcely good
enough for him to set his foot on. During our innocent
lunch of bread and jam and milk we heard him loudly
ordering his, which was rather extensive, and ended with
champagne, and haranguing violently against Ireland.

"It's a wretched country, and the Irish are such a discontented lot, they'd never be satisfied with anything we"
(oh, that magnificent *we !*) " gave them."

Here the Yankee tried to put in a good word, but was
quickly annihilated.

"You Americans are just as bad. You back Ireland in
all her rebellion. And what are you yourselves? Only
'third class.' You've no gentlemen among you. And your
ladies—they're not bad-looking, but they get old in no
time; after five-and-twenty they haven't a tooth in their
heads."

Here the much-enduring American blazed up. " Sir,
I could tell you a few things about your English ladies, if
there were not some of them present—"

We never heard the end of the sentence, for we rose at
once and departed—the three girls burning with indigna-

tion. Age takes things more calmly than youth; but I determined, as a warning to travellers, to write down *verbatim*
the conversation of these two men. I know nothing of
either—not even their names—but they deserve to be thus
anonymously pilloried: it cannot harm them, and may do
them good. The slow-brained, overbearing, money-loving
Saxon is of all things most repellent to the proud, irascible,
impassioned Celt. Neither can comprehend the other's
virtues, while all their faults are obnoxiously clear. No
wonder that England finds it so difficult to govern Ireland.

We were getting a little hot ourselves over the never-
ending question of race—equally balanced between us four
—when the scale was turned by the sudden appearance of
a fifth addition to our party; whom, following the same
system of *lucus a non lucendo*, I will entitle the Barbarous
Scot. Middle-aged but merry, pleasant and paternal, the
three girls hailed him with enthusiasm. He had travelled
without stopping for thirty-six hours, yet was in the best
of spirits, determined to enjoy everything.

Apparently he had thought there was little or nothing
to be enjoyed, for he looked round the hotel with an air of
mild surprise, "Why, you are quite comfortable!"

Certainly we were—even in the far north of Ireland.
We had all that travellers could need, and some things
which they seldom get—a charming drawing-room and a
first-rate piano. Also, hear it not, ghosts of Fin MacCoul
and the Gray Man!—there was actually between us and
the wild Atlantic—an asphalte lawn-tennis ground!

The Barbarous Scot eyed everything with great content; and then made the very natural inquiry, " And where is the Giant's Causeway ?"

He was taken thither, not by sea—he had had enough of that—but down the steep path, which is really the best way to see it, and from which the groups of midday tourists had all disappeared, leaving the place as silent and solitary as heart could desire.

Equally so was the high cliff-walk, eastward towards the Pleaskin, and looking down on the Causeway, with its surroundings of strange-shaped rocks and boiling sea between—on this coast it seems as if the sea could never be quiet—while turning westward you could see the clear curve of the distant coast—part Donegal, part Derry—with Malin Head at the farthest point. Beyond was the ocean, which at the north of Ireland still looks as desolate as in the time of the mythical giants or foreign marauders, Picts and Scots, as much barbarians as the Irish race they attacked and vainly tried to conquer.

As I watched the sun drop down, a red ball of fire, into the Atlantic, it was easy to imagine the past, and difficult to go back into the present, an excellent *table d' hôte* and polite conversation—which to our amazement we saw going on at the farther end of the table between John Bull and the American. They must have settled their little difficulty, and agreed that " Live and let live " is the best motto for opposing nationalities as well as individuals.

By the time we went up into the drawing-room the wind and sea had risen, and were howling outside like a thousand demons. Windows rattled, doors shook: we could hardly hear ourselves speak. But the fire burned brightly, as if it had been December instead of August; the jest and the laugh went round; we all felt so happy and "at home" that it was difficult to believe we were sitting in a strange hotel at the utmost north of Ireland.

August 26th.—And the most hopeless day imaginable! The storm had abated—the girls declared they had actually felt their beds shaking during the night; but daybreak brought calm, and a downpour of rain that seemed as if it would never cease. A visit to the electric tramway between Portrush and Bushmills, and to Dunluce Castle, which we had arranged with our kind stranger-friend overnight, became impracticable. However, we had letters to write; and found that we could communicate with the outer world by telegraph as easily here as we could at home. So we settled ourselves stoically in-doors—leaving the Barbarous Scot, who of all things detests doing nothing, to enjoy himself under a mackintosh outside, or stand inside, with a field-glass, intently contemplating something in the far distance—perhaps New York.

At noon it began to clear — Irish weather does clear in the most extraordinary way, when you least expect it. Our original plan was vain; but half a day was too much to lose—so we decided on revisiting Carrick-a-rede, which the girls declared they had only half seen in the dim twilight two days before.

It was a gray day still, with occasional droppings of rain; but we determined to enjoy it. We pointed out to the Barbarous Scot all the places we had already seen—Dunseverick, which looked grand against the dull gray sky, and which he allowed was one of the finest old castles he had ever beheld; Ballintoy, which he considered "a wretched hole," as perhaps it was. But the ragged inhabitants, who came out to look at us, only looked; not one of them begged, as, alas! is often done in Ireland—and elsewhere. And when we alighted, to walk past the large quarries in the open cliff, the quarrymen were very civil, and the man with a flag who hurried us on—as they were waiting to "blast" until we had gone by—did his duty as considerately as possible.

When we paused, out of breath, and deafened by the explosion behind us, the Barbarous Scot, who evidently thought he had been brought a long and difficult road to see nothing, demanded—as some readers may also demand —"And what *is* Carrick-a-rede?"

Carrick-a-rede is an isolated rock separated from the mainland by a deep chasm of about sixty feet across—the island itself being ninety feet above the level of the sea. Over this chasm is a bridge, so slight that in our artist's sketch it is invisible. It is made with two ropes—barred by transverse pieces of wood so as to form a footway. A third rope is used as a guide-rope for the hand. Across this perilous bridge the fisher-folk—men, women, and children—pass and repass; often carrying heavy weights, as the island is an excellent place for salmon-fishing. One false step and down they would go into the boiling sea, which makes a perpetual whirlpool through this narrow channel.

CARRICK-A-REDE BY MOONLIGHT.
(*From a Drawing by* F. NOEL PATON.)

When we reached the spot three men were preparing to cross, one at a time, as the bridge swings so, the footway seeming to swing one way and the guide-rope another. Also, the island being somewhat higher than the cliff-side opposite, there were several feet of a steep slope before reaching the centre of the bridge. And the noise and roar of the waters below dashing themselves against black, jagged rocks—it turned one dizzy to look and to listen. But the three men crossed, one after the other, with complete indifference, and ascended the ladder—which was fixed against the rocky point where we stood—laughing and joking among themselves.

"Ay, ay, ma'am," said one whom I spoke to—an elderly man—"it needs a bit o' care an' a steady foot. But we're used to it. We begin it as children, and then we're all right."

"Does no one ever fall?"

He paused a minute. "A year ago a man went over. But he was hearty."

Hearty, we found, is the local euphemism for *drunk.* "And of course he was drowned?"

The fisherman pointed to the whirlpool below. "Couldn't live two minutes, *there.*"

"Did you get his body?"

A shake of the head only. "Knocked to bits—sure to be," said the fisherman, as he shouldered his bundle—nets, I think; but each of the three men carried something—and marched off up the steep hillside. These Antrim men have the Scottish characteristic of speaking but little, and seldom unless spoken to.

After that we watched more men come across, six in all, and then our three girls descended the cliff-ladder. One, the Violet, being "young and foolish," set her foot on the first step of the bridge—but wisely drew back again. We wondered if our artist, who we knew had been there, had crossed it.

"Depend upon it he has! No active young fellow could resist the pleasure of doing it," said the Barbarous Scot.

I said I hoped this young fellow would have the sense to resist doing a foolhardy thing, except for duty or necessity. The girls, having no data to go upon, argued the point

in the abstract; and thence ensued one of those ethical
conversations over which we were wont to beguile the time
—sometimes fighting so energetically that we quite forgot
what we were fighting about. (We afterwards found that
this dispute was like that of the two knights on either side
of the shield. Our artist, when questioned, replied com-
posedly, " Oh, yes; the island was the best point for sketching; so I crossed." But I would advise most tourists to
think twice before venturing upon the bridge of Carrick-a-
rede.)

It was growing late—yet we lingered; listening to the
roar of the waves below, and looking at the sea beyond—
wide and blank, except for two islands. One, Sheep
Island, was a mere dot on the water. There is a superstition that only twelve sheep can be pastured upon it; if
thirteen are landed there, they starve; if eleven, they over-
eat themselves and die. Rathlin Island, lying like a narrow
fish on the top of the water, five miles distant from the
shore, is a curious place—of which we afterwards heard a
good deal.

An anonymous writer, two centuries back, calling it by
its ancient name of Raghery—describes it as " shaped like
an Irish stocking, the toe of which pointeth to the mainland." It is five miles long by half a mile broad; very
rocky to the westward—some rocks taking the columnar
form as at the Causeway — while the eastern slope is fertile
and cultivated. Its inhabitants, once about fifteen hundred, are now not more than five hundred souls—exclusively farmers and fishermen. They speak a combination of

Irish and Scottish Gaelic, but very little English; and are a distinct and remarkable race, hardy, daring, and superstitious; and clinging closely to their old history, or tradition, for it is not easy to divide the two.

The quantity of human bones found on the island implies that it must have been the scene of many a forgotten battle; and the islanders speak with a wrath as hot as if it had happened yesterday of a massacre about the time of Elizabeth, when all the women living there, except one, whose name was McCurdy, were flung over the rocks into the sea. But the only visible relics of antiquity are a part of the cliffs still called "the White Palace," where a Norwegian king is said to have courted the daughter of an Irish chieftain; and "Bruce's Castle"—a mere fragment—supposed to be one of the many refuges of that great Scottish hero.

Visitors to Rathlin are few, as the only communication between it and Ballycastle, the nearest point to the mainland, is by open boat; and narrow as the channel is, sometimes it cannot be crossed for days or weeks.

Its fauna and flora are said to be interesting. There are no frogs — which, spite of St. Patrick, have crept into the mainland — but there are wild goats, Cornish choughs, gyrfalcons, and abundance of puffins and guillemots. Two tiny fresh-water lakes furnish some rare lacustrine plants. In fact, Rathlin would be a desirable spot for any tourist who was not particular about his accommodation—and indifferent as to the length of time he stayed.

Though boasting a priest and a parson, it is said to be

happily free of both doctors and lawyers. The only administrator of justice is Mr. Gage, the owner of the island, and a permanent resident there. Being a legally appointed J.P., he settles all disputes among the innocent and peaceful inhabitants, to whom he is—report declares—an excellent landlord. So, on the whole, Rathlin may be considered a happy island.

We regarded it with longing, though to visit it would, we felt, be impracticable. But those adventurous souls who do so may be sure of the pleasure which there always is in investigating an almost unknown place, where everything is strange and new.

The fishermen who came from Carrick-a-rede told us we could reach the main road without recrossing the quarries; so we went. It was a stiff climb, up a slippery, grassy slope. I sat and rested at the roadside while the others went on to send back the car from Ballintoy; amusing myself with watching two beautiful white goats that were tethered near a cottage — out of which soon came the mistress. She looked, as to her clothes, what in England would be called "a bundle of rags"—but had a bright, clean, smiling face, and the pleasant manner which you seldom miss in Ireland.

"Ye'll be looking at my goats, ma'am? They're bonnie craythurs, aren't they? And they give such a lot o' milk."

I said I supposed they served instead of a cow.

"'Deed, an' we couldn't keep a cow—any of us. She'd eat too much. But these eat very little"—patting the snowy necks of her goats, who seemed to know her well—

"an' their milk's wondherful. D'ye know, ma'am," looking in my face with a simple confidence which was quite
touching, "I made three pounds of butther last week—
besides the milk for the childher."

I expressed surprise and congratulation, and then her
sympathy flowed towards me.

"Ye're looking tired, ma'am. Ye'll have been to Carrick-a-rede? It's a steep brae"—so many Scottish words
and phrases, I noted, were current here—"Will I fetch you
a chair? or would ye come inside? or maybe ye'd like a
drink o' milk?"

"Inside" was an abode about as large and not so well-
built as that of my pig at home. And I had tasted goat's
milk once—but have no intention of doing it twice. Nevertheless the hospitality was declined—I trust—as gratefully
as if it had come from a palace. We stood a long time
talking together, and admiring the goats, till she at last
bade me "Good-day" with cheerful politeness, and took her
"craythurs" with her into the cabin — which, no doubt,
they shared with the rest of the family. And yet "John
Bull" that morning had declared that the Irish were always discontented!

I allow, there is a wholesome discontent which rouses
into amendment, and there is a lazy content which ends in
hunger and rags. But between these two lies a happy
medium. And I must say, throughout the north of Ireland
I was less struck by the poverty than by the cheerfulness
with which it is borne.

The gray day had brightened into a splendid evening,

and we drove back westward, facing one of the grandest
sea-sunsets I ever saw. At the hotel door we found waiting two of the many kind stranger-friends who seemed to
turn up everywhere. From them we gained no end of
information, and spent with them one of those social accidental evenings which are the true enjoyment of travelling;
when both sides have to break into absolutely new ground,
and find therein much that they never expected to find, but
can warmly appreciate when found.

August 27th.—As usual, the bad day was followed by
one so gorgeous that we said at once, "What a day for
Dunluce!"

"And for the electric railway," added the Barbarous
Scot, who is mechanically - minded, and had been filling
his soul overnight with turbines, dynamos, and what not.
But as I do not understand these things, and have received so often the humiliating advice, "Don't let your
ignorance be known," I will not commit myself to any
scientific explanations.

However, I may safely say a word or two about this
railway, which is the great feature of the district, and the
key which may unlock its resources to both pleasure and
commerce.

About 1881 Sir William Siemens, Sir William Thomson,
and Mr. W. A. Traill, all men of practical scientific knowledge, and the two latter connected by birth with the north
of Ireland, conceived the idea of opening up the country,
utilizing labor, and bringing in capital, by means of an

7

electric tramway, to extend from Portrush to the Giant's Causeway, and to be worked by the abundant water-power of the river Bush, at a salmon leap near Bushmills. It was to be constructed on a raised footway along the main road —a very good one, which runs close by the coast.

Enormous opposition arose—as is often the case with suggested improvements in Ireland. The principal land-owners, and the directors of the Northern Counties Railway, set themselves equally against it. Into their reasons, or motives, it is needless to enter; since, as nothing succeeds like success, probably all these excellent gentlemen will have changed their minds by now. But at the time they were a great hinderance to what outsiders would have considered a permanent benefit to the country.

"I must distinctly state," one who had knowledge of the facts said to me, "that under any system of local self-government, guided by local prejudices, the originators of the tramway would never have been able to carry it through. Only by applying to an unbiassed, extraneous tribunal such as the imperial Parliament could they have succeeded in attaining their end."

But it was attained. They got their bills passed, their railway constructed, and on the 28th of September, 1883, it was opened by the viceroy, Earl Spencer, as far as Bushmills. This winter of 1886–7 it will be opened to the Giant's Causeway—that is, to the hotel grounds, a distance of eight miles. One of the most energetic of its projectors has passed away without seeing its completion: Sir William Siemens died almost immediately after the day of opening, when was gathered together, besides many scientific men, a host of friends; whose sympathy—and money, which almost entirely came from a distance—had been given from the first.

The tramway was constructed entirely by local workmen; which was one of the important ends desired to be accomplished. Not without difficulty, for the typical Irishman, at least in his own country, has to be taught to work. He will stand, spade in hand, for a certain number of hours, then throw it down, and consider that he has given his employer a fair day's work for a fair day's wages. The rule of what we call in England piece-work—that is, payment for the amount of work done, not the time it takes to do it—is to him almost unknown. The gangers on this railway had not only to tell their men what to do, but to show them how to do it, and see that they did it, for most of them were mere agricultural laborers of the most ignorant kind.

Notable exceptions, however, there were, when the ingrained quickness of the Irish brain—so valuable, if only it is united to perseverance—showed itself here and there, conquering every difficulty. The present electrician, who overlooks the dynamos, was the engineer's coachman, who had no previous knowledge of electricity whatever, and the man who attends to the turbines and generators was a farm laborer, taken on at the age of eighteen, when the tramway was begun, and working his way up to his present position — a very important one. He has to remain at the "generating station," at Bushmills, and regulate the water

that drives the enormous electric dynamos, one of which
weighs five tons, and has had seven miles of copper wire
used in its construction.   Yet the machinery is so delicate
that the indicators on the wall tell him the precise moment when a train leaves Portrush ; the amount of electricity which is being used enabling him to calculate to
a nicety the weight and speed of the cars, so that he can
supply the turbines with more or less water to meet the
strain required on any point of the journey.

The intelligent conscientiousness of this young man,
upon whom so much depends, contrasts pleasantly with
the narrow-minded ignorance of others, chiefly carters and
car-drivers, who often wantonly injure the railway, from
a foolish notion that it is injuring them.   Anything like
progress is difficult to be comprehended by an uneducated
race ; and the apparent simplicity of the lines of railway
—unprotected, except by a low hand-rail, and a warning
" not to touch "—roused the dangerous curiosity of passers-
by.   Many comical stories are told—of an old woman who
sat down, basket and all, upon the hand-rail, and slipped
backwards into a low quarry behind ; and a horse, which
having strayed and fallen across the rails, when lifted
up by the tail, gave out shocks of electricity through his
whole body to such an extent that his rescuers took to
their heels and ran away.

But though it is good to impress upon the ignorant
country folk not to meddle with the mysterious railway, there is practically little or no danger in it, even exposed as it is.   The power required to propel two or three

cars, with fifty or sixty passengers, absorbs so much of the electric current as to render it harmless to chance touches; and when little work has to be done the tension is kept so low that only a very slight shock could be felt. Sometimes people are seen amusing themselves by holding hands in a ring, to "see what will happen"—but, as no harm ever has happened, we may safely hope none ever will.

These facts, gathered from an entirely reliable source, we learned afterwards, but this forenoon all we noticed was the single line of rails, guarded by a low hand-rail which ran alongside of the main road where we were driving. We stopped, as the cars stop, at the little wicket gate leading to Dunluce Castle.

This many-pinnacled sea-fortress is one of the most picturesque ruins I ever saw. It is built on a rock like Dunseverick, but is not near so ancient; the earliest mention of it being in the time of the Tudors, when it was taken from the native McQuillans by the Scottish McDonnells. The story runs that a young McDonnell came over to help McQuillan in his wars with the savage tribes round him; spent a winter at Dunluce, and at the end of it ran away with his host's daughter, married her, and based upon that marriage a claim to the castle and all the land. Since then the McQuillans have partially died out, though the name is not quite extinct, but the McDonnells still populate the whole country-side.

However, the fact with which some of our party consoled ourselves, that probably half of these respected ancestors were hanged, and the other half ought to have been, did not prevent us from enjoying the soft sunshine which bathed every nook or corner of the old castle, which had seen so much bloodshed in it or near it.

It is in two distinct parts, the remains of the stables and servants' offices being on the mainland, while the castle itself is on an isolated rock, crossed by a grass-edged footbridge no wider than a plank. Many rooms are still distinguishable, among the rest the Banshee's Chamber, which has the peculiarity of being always clean, some curious current of air sweeping every particle of dust from the floor. The Banshee, usually a female ancestress of the family, was in this case the daughter of a cruel father who imprisoned her in this chamber; trying to escape thence by means of a rope-ladder, she and her lover both were drowned. So, of stormy nights she is still heard, weeping and wailing in this tiny room.

Nothing, I think, strikes one more in examining old castles than the miserable smallness of the domestic apartments in which our forefathers passed their time. The banqueting-rooms were grand, the kitchens enormous, but the family must have lived and slept anyhow and anywhere.

The clever mediæval workmen who built these walls, fitted them so ingeniously to the very edge of the cliff that they look like a continuation of the rock itself, especially near the Tinker's Corner — which is shown as the spot where one stormy Christmas night a travelling tinker made his bed, much to the annoyance of the servants of the castle.

However, before morning, a sudden hurricane blew the kitchen wall, and eleven people with it, right into the sea below—the poor tinker alone escaping.

But one might find—or make—endless legends about Dunluce; which is said to have been inhabited as late as the year 1750. Now it lies desolate, except during the brief hour or two when Belfast people make "a day out" and roam about it—or stray tourists like ourselves go peering in and out, and gazing from the windowless windows, as the Banshee lady, or more determined McDonnell maiden, must have done, in the days when women were mere appendages to men, as daughters, sisters, wives to fathers, brothers, and husbands, to be fought for, or bargained for, as occasion served.

My three girls, with their hearts and their lives in their own hands, free and merry, busy and content, were in some things a happy contrast to the fair damsels of former days. They wandered about as much as they wished; then we forsook the ancient for the modern, and devoted ourselves to the examination of the great mystery of the future—electricity.

The salmon-leap on the river Bush is an extremely pretty waterfall which science has converted into most satisfactory ugliness by means of certain extraordinary machines called "turbines"—the use of which my readers, I hope, know or can find out, for I dare not attempt to explain. Close by is a deafening engine-room, which the resident engineer, Mr. Traill, regarded with the utmost tenderness, as he did every portion of his work. To his enthusiastic energy, combined with perseverance, the electric railway owes nearly all its success.

When we arrived, he and two of his men were digging at a small hole close above the waterfall.

"We've found it!" he said (something had gone wrong, and the cars yesterday had been obliged to be drawn by the tramway-engine, kept permanently for the goods traffic). "I have traced it all the way from Portrush, and have just come upon the flaw. We shall put it right and be in working order to-morrow."

Which seemed to us a wonderful thing, until we remembered hearing how, soon after the laying of the first Atlantic telegraph, a similar flaw was discovered and traced for thousands of miles at the bottom of the sea. These secrets of Nature, discoverable to science, always strike the uninitiated mind with a sense of the marvellous, which appeals strongly to the imagination. Little as we understood of its working, we could not but feel the advantage the electric railway was likely to be in this district, if the people have sense to accept the advance of civilization, of which it is a token, and use the resources of the country, which have so long lain dormant. That this was not always so is evident from a discovery made more than a century ago by two men "pushing an adit," as it is called, in the coal-fields of Ballycastle. They came upon an ancient mine, and for more than twelve hours wandered among a labyrinth of passages—thirty-six distinct chambers, fashioned with a skill equal to that of the present day. They also found baskets, mining instruments, and other relics of workers whose labor must have ended, perhaps, a thousand years ago—for there is no record whatever, either in history or tradition, of this mysterious mine.

Thus the tide of civilization sweeps backward and forward, advancing and retiring, over the whole world; and the utmost we petty men can do is to take it at the turn, and make the best use of it.

We took our last walk along the beautiful cliff, and spent our last evening in the pleasant drawing-room, thinking how delightful would be a Christmas week at the Causeway Hotel, with the wind blowing and the waves roaring—almost as good as being at sea, yet with a safe footing on *terra firma.* Those seven windows looking on Blackrock Strand, Dunluce Castle, Ramore Head, with the Donegal Mountains behind, would furnish a landscape unsurpassable in the three kingdoms.

Also—which is not to be despised, amid all the outside beauty—to be thoroughly comfortable within doors, well-warmed, well-housed, well-fed, well-lighted (with the electric light, which is to be brought up from the railway this winter), might attract those who do not care for higher things. Lovers of the grand and beautiful, artists and archæologists, will go through any hardships to gain their delights; but even lovers of creature comforts might do worse than spend a few—or a good many—delightful days at the Giant's Causeway.

Note.—On repeating this wish to "one who knows"—being a resident close by—he smiled grimly. " Well, it's a

matter of taste. We have a hurricane about once a fortnight; our skylights are occasionally smashed, the hotel
is entirely dismantled from October to April, and the
seven windows you couldn't well look out of; they have
to be boarded up, or they would be blown in." So I am
obliged to recant, and must not advise anybody to winter
at the Giant's Causeway.

PART IV.

STEAM after all, and not electricity, took us to Portrush. The flaw, discovered with such ingenuity and mended next day, was, alas! not mended till seven P.M—and we had to depart at five. So we started—by the locomotive always kept in readiness for such emergencies, which, however, seldom happen. The worst that can happen is that the electric current fails, and the train stops. No collisions, explosions, and other disasters, that most railway lines are exposed to, are possible on this line. Whether its motive power would be available for greater distances, and at the speed which modern travellers require, is for future engineers to discover and determine.

But of the beauty, safety, and convenience of this eight-mile electric railway, there can be no doubt. Carried entirely along the common main road, it skirts the sea so closely that you can look out of the carriage windows and see below you the waves dashing among the rocks, chiefly of black basalt, except the White Rocks, which are of dazzling limestone. Everywhere they take the strangest

forms; are beaten into caves and archways, through which
the ever-restless waters come pouring and boiling; while
here and there are tiny bays, bordered by a few yards of
smooth sand, and sheltered overhead by dizzy cliffs, where
the steadiest head and the surest foot would hardly venture
to climb.

A last glance at Dunluce, with its many-peaked ruins
clear against the afternoon sky—a restless jumping up and
down every minute to see some bit of coast, each more
beautiful than the last — and we found ourselves back in
civilization; for the electric cars run right through the
principal street of Portrush to the railway station which
connects that town with Belfast, Coleraine, Londonderry,
and southern Ireland.

And here I wish to say a word or two, "more in sorrow
than in anger," about Irish railways, as they strike an accidental traveller who is neither a landowner, a railway direc-
tor, a government official, nor a political demagogue, but,
as I have said—only a woman.

The last generation set up its Conservative back against
all railways, as being sure to spoil the look of the country,
to interfere with its local trade and local rights—and plant
Demos, with all his unpleasant belongings, under the very
nose of Aristos. The present generation is wiser. It has
discovered that after a railway is once made, Nature re-
coups herself for any temporary destruction with marvellous rapidity. She clothes blasted rocks with ferns, turns
ugly embankments into grassy slopes, and plants there, in
a year or two, mile-long beds of primroses and cowslips.

Between station and station, a line of railway leaves the country nearly as lonely and beautiful as it found it—except for the occasional apparition of that long black serpent with its two fiery eyes, and its trail of white steam and black smoke, winding through a wide champaign, or darting in and out of cuttings and tunnels, like a thing alive.

No doubt the locomotive has been a wonderful engine of civilization. Even in regions where its entrance appears most cruel—such as the English lakes and the Highlands of Scotland—it has done more good than harm. But in Ireland it seems to do more harm than good; being so mismanaged and misused that one longs to go back to the common road and outside car.

I do not hesitate to say that of all railways I ever travelled by, in England, Scotland, France, Switzerland, Italy, the Irish railways are the very worst. People give as a reason for this that the rival companies are always squabbling, and seem to take pleasure in making their train-service *not* fit in, so that at important junctions one train often departs just three minutes before another arrives—a system of "cutting off your nose to spite your face" which is, alas! only too common in Ireland. Also, the great poverty of the country is made to account for the fact that the carriages are often at the lowest ebb of shabbiness and even dangerous decay; the officials are underpaid, and therefore incompetent and few. As for the railway stations—I never entered a single one, in large towns, small towns, or country places, that was not, to English notions of cleanliness, a perfect pigsty! Civility was never lacking—never is in Ireland; for instance, once at an important junction, where I had to wait two hours and could not even find a decent bench to sit down upon, a sympathetic porter politely put me into an empty first-class carriage that was shunted aside till wanted. But as for punctuality, order, and that commonest decent tidiness of platforms, booking-offices, and waiting-rooms — which would only cost a few shillings weekly in brushes and brooms, soap and water—these things are absolutely unattainable.

There may be exceptions, but, as a rule, between the want of money and the reckless expenditure of it — inherent laziness on the one hand, and on the other the fatal national peculiarity of fighting over a grievance instead of joining hand-in-hand to remedy it — the Irish railway system is apparently rotten to the core. If government, as I heard suggested, would take the whole network of lines into its own hands, and work them upon a system of unity instead of opposition, it would greatly benefit the shareholders, the travellers, and the country at large. At present, this most important element in the prosperity of any land—its means of public locomotion—is like a body without a head, a household without a master, and nothing but strong, firm, conscientious rule, that righteous authority which only the unrighteous need fear, will ever put things right.

Having said thus much — individualizing nothing and nobody, but with the earnest hope that it may "meet the eye" of those whom it concerns—I will leave the subject.

Portrush, of which we saw only the railway station, is called "the Queen of Ulster watering-places." It boasts a grand hotel, with many others less grand, a fashionable promenade on Ramore Head, and many other delights which we did not care for, though doubtless we should have found some that we did. But on the whole we were content to pass through it, for the sake of a Sunday at Londonderry.

At Coleraine we found not the traditional "Kitty of Coleraine," but a crowd of very unbeautiful "Kittys," rushing hither and thither as female country people usually do at a junction where there is nobody to direct them. We too felt somewhat bewildered, in the great lack of officials to tell us where to go and what to do; but at last succeeded in being safely shut into a decent carriage, as was the chief aim of the Barbarous Scot—I think it is of most Scotsmen—all to ourselves, with none of our obnoxious fellow-creatures beside us.

So we steamed away slowly, very slowly, for the line between Coleraine and Derry, though short in distance, is long in time. But it is a rarely beautiful line, running a little way along the sea-coast, then crossing a triangular peninsula, then skirting the edge of Lough Foyle, mile after mile; often actually carried upon piles across the water, which lay smooth in the golden sunset, with a line of low hills as background. A pretty spot, and much appreciated, for we passed clusters of "genteel villas," the inhabitants of which, late as was the hour, were disporting themselves like mermaids in the lough. And as

8

it narrowed to a mere river, we could see, sitting on the top of its picturesque hill,

"The little town of Derry, not a league from Culmore Ferry"

—but not a little town now; for it extends far beyond the walls, along the valley and up the slope, where, two hundred years ago, lay encamped the besieging Franco-Irish army of King James II.

Londonderry can scarcely be called an unknown country, yet tourists so seldom visit it that our landlady apologized kindly for any lack of comfort by saying she was only accustomed to "commercial gentlemen"—whom we observed "taking their ease at their inn" in the best room of the house. However, we were too tired to grumble—nay, while I rested the four others valorously went out into the town and amused themselves with the humors of a Saturday-night crowd—such a contrast to the life alone with Nature, which we had led for two weeks.

Next morning we saw the sun shining on the trees in the bishop's garden — and prepared for a pleasant day. A kindly missive from friends advised us to go to the Church of St. Augustine on the walls, as the cathedral was under repair. So we went, lingering on the way to look at the monument erected to the Rev. George Walker, who was Governor of Londonderry during the siege, and whose curious and authentic account of it we had bought in the town for the sum of sixpence.

Derry—or Londonderry, as it was called after being rebuilt at the expense of the City of London, in 1633—is one of the prettiest towns in Ireland. Its encircling walls, and four gateways, form the pleasantest of walks, whence you can see the country for miles and miles—on one side, smiling pasture-lands, and low hills; on the other, the glittering length of Lough Foyle. We stood a long time by Walker's monument and statue, thinking of that siege of Derry, which is still such a vivid and bitter political memory in Ulster; but which ordinary English people know so little about that a few words concerning it may not come amiss.

In the struggle between Catholics and Protestants, the deposed James II. on the one side, and William and Mary of Orange on the other, there was no fiercer battle-ground than the province of Ulster and the city of Londonderry. Its inhabitants—composed chiefly of English Episcopalians and Scottish Presbyterians—when James and his Franco-Irish army of twenty thousand men appeared, summoning them to surrender, preferred to fight. They drove away from among them all the native Irish, shut their gates, and sustained for a hundred and five days a siege ever memorable, both for the courage of the besieged and their cruel sufferings. Between April and August nine thousand of them died—more from famine and sickness than from the enemy, who sat all the while on the hillside opposite, battering the city at intervals, or trying by treachery to enter there. In one instance nine prentice lads, seeing the French soldiers within sixty yards of the gate—which had been opened for a parley—seized the keys, ran down, and locked it only just in time.

The miseries of the townpeople were great. Governor

Walker gives a list of food, and its price: "One pound of horse-flesh, 1s. 8d. A quarter of a dog, fatned [*sic*] by eating the Bodies of the slain Irish, 2s. 6d. A Rat, 1s. A Mouse, sixpence. And," he adds, with terrible simplicity, "we had nothing left to eat unless we could prey upon one another. A certain Fat gentleman conceived himself in greatest danger. Fancying the garrison lookt at him with a greedy Eye, he thought fit to hide himself for three Days."

In this dire extremity, when the living were half dead, and the dead had been buried by hundreds, under streets and in back yards, anywhere where a little earth could be got to cover them — often so little that a bomb entering would tear it up again, and disclose all the horrors of the new-made grave — two ships, which they knew were laden with food, appeared sailing up the lough to relieve the town. Mrs. Alexander, wife of the present Bishop of Derry, has told the story in a poem lately published—which for beauty and power is surely destined to become, like her "Burial of Moses," an English classic.

> "Like a falcon on her perch, our fair Cathedral church
>   Above the tide-vext river looks eastward from the bay;
> Dear namesake of St. Columb! and each morning, sweet and solemn,
>   The bells through all the tumult have called on us to pray.

> "Our leader speaks the prayer, the captains are all there;
>   His deep voice never falters though his look be sad and grave,
> On the women's pallid faces, and the soldiers in their places,
>   And the stones above our brothers that lie buried in the nave.

> "They are closing round us still by the river; on the hill
>   You can see the white pavilions round the standards of their chief,
> But the Lord is up in heaven, though the chances are uneven,
>   Though the boom is in the river whence we looked for our relief."

The "boom" was a huge mast, tied across the river with ropes, to hinder the food-ships from passing to the water-gate. The little *Mountjoy,* trying to force it, was met by a rain of cannon-balls, one of which cut the rope, and the concussion, setting her afloat, for she was nearly stranded, she passed safely over the boom.

> "She sails up to the town, like a queen in a white gown,
>   And golden are her lilies, true gold are all her men:
>   Now the *Phœnix* follows after, I can hear the women's laughter,
>   And the shouting of the soldiers till the echoes ring again."

So complete was the rescue that King James's army melted away in a few days from before the town. Derry was saved.

It was strange to stand on the walls listening to the peaceful Sabbath bells and watch the good people going into church—the pretty little church which has been built on the site of an Augustinian monastery—and think of all the scenes enacted there only two centuries ago. How the world has changed!—except that there still lies smouldering everywhere in northern Ireland the embers of that fierce religious hatred, begun in the time of Queen Elizabeth, and continued down to the present day.

But long before then, in times absolutely without record, Derry must have been a favorite fighting-ground. Its great natural advantages, seated on a hill at the head of the lough, and commanding such an extent of country, by water and land, probably made it an inhabited settlement coeval with the Grainan Aileach, or palace of the ancient Irish kings in the north, as Tara was in the south.

This curious "remain," with its circular wall thirteen feet thick, and its massive entrance-gate, is still to be seen on a hillside four miles from Londonderry. Some antiquaries, judging from both traditionary and internal evidence, date it as far back as a thousand years before Christ. But, at any rate, it is mentioned in the "Annals of the Four Masters" some centuries after Christ, as a very ancient building plundered by the Danes, and finally demolished by Murtagh O'Brien, King of Munster, who ordered each of his men to bring a stone from Grainan Aileach back to Limerick.

Of this palace there is still enough left to distinguish the line of three earthen ramparts and terraces of stones, adjusted to fit in to one another without cement. I can only describe it from hearsay—for I never saw it; though it was the place which of all others I should have liked to see.

After church we, with the help of kind friends, utilized every minute, and succeeded, I think, in taking in most of the points connected with that episode in history of which Derry seems most proud—its lengthened siege and almost miraculous deliverance.

Our first visit was to the cathedral, under the charge of two of its dignitaries, one of whom was making his weekly progress among scaffolding and workmen's *débris*, to see how its restoration was advancing. His earnest enthusiasm over it reminded us of the old mediæval days when people spent their whole lives and incomes in building cathedrals "for the glory of God."

Derry Cathedral is not ancient, dating only from 1622, as recorded in a tablet on the wall.

> " If stones could speake
> Then London's prayse
> Should sound. Who
> Built this Church and
> Cittie from the grounde."

Consequently it is only a church, has no cloisters, no close, as in Catholic times, when the monastery and cathedral were often combined.   King Charles I. presented to it its peal of bells, and dedicated it to St. Columb or Columba, who a thousand years before had here instituted one of his bishoprics, which held so important a position in the early history of Ireland.

The British laity in general are little aware of the facts, proved as far as any ancient historical facts can be, that at a time when England was sunk in Druidic barbarism, or struggling madly with Saxons, Danes, and Normans, Ireland was very fairly civilized, and its Church was a Christian Church, with a clear form of ecclesiastical government —bishops, priests, abbots.   In a very early Irish poem, a saint, coeval with St. Patrick, is thus referred to :

" Not poor was the family [*i. e.*, monastic family] of St. Mochta, of Louth's fort.   Three hundred priests and one hundred bishops along with him, and threescore singing elders, composed his royal, noble household.   They ploughed not, they reaped not, they dried not corn ; they labored not, save at learning only."

But St. Columba — or Columbkille — Columba of the

Church as he was afterwards called — seems to have had other pursuits than learning. Born at Garton in Donegal, of royal blood, he was politician and soldier as well as priest, and, embroiling himself with his kinsmen, had to fly from Derry, then called Derry Columbkille. He took refuge in Iona, where he built another cathedral, and instituted a new system of ecclesiastical polity among the semi-barbarous Picts and Scots. Tradition, and the archæological remains still existing at Staffa and Iona, and all along these northern isles, show to what an extent he must have both civilized and Christianized them. St. Columba never returned to Ireland, but died in his cathedral at Iona, one midnight, in front of the high-altar, at the ripe age of seventy-seven. His influence, both within and without the Church, must have been enormous; and his charter, strong, firm, and just, accounts for it. The form of Church government which he originated subsisted for several centuries in Ireland. One of its remarkable features was the respect paid and the authority given to women —for instance, the abbess St. Brigid, or Bridget, seems to have been a friend of St. Columba, consulted by him on many occasions, and possessing almost equal influence with himself in matters ecclesiastical.

Derry Cathedral is too modern to have any relics of saints or ancient tombs — indeed, its history begins with Puritanism. The first curiosity we were shown was a cannon-ball fired into the town, containing a letter, offering a large reward to whoever should open the gates to King James's army outside. But in vain. Apparently, the only

"Mr. Feeble-mind" in Derry was its bishop, Ezekiel Hopkins, who, after giving it its communion plate and organ, retired south for safety, and ended his days as a poor curate of a London church. It was for the humble minister of Donoughmore—the Reverend George Walker—to exchange cassock for sword, and make himself notable forever as the Governor of Derry during its terrible siege.

The cathedral is full of reminiscences of that cruel time. We were shown an opening, only lately discovered by the workmen, leading by an underground passage to the sallyport. And when, in 1861, the paving had to be taken up, under it was found a dense mass, three feet deep, of human bones, mingled with fragments of silken ribbon, which was distinctly seen to be of that orange color that for two centuries has been in Ireland the fatal signal—as fatal now as ever—of political and religious warfare. After much careless desecration, the spirit of the townsfolk was at last roused; and these poor bones of the brave defenders of Derry were reverently collected and reburied. That none might be lost, even the earth dug out near them was piled into a mound outside, with an inscription that records almost too bitterly the feeling of their descendants.

A wholesome lesson upon this—the undying animosity between Protestant and Catholic—was the bishop's sermon, which we went to hear in the town-hall; where, during the restoration of the cathedral, service is conducted. His text—"Now the fruit of the Spirit is love, joy, and peace"—was expounded with a power and earnestness worthy of one of the best preachers in the Irish Church, as he is held

to be. Ornate—perhaps a little too ornate, but the Celtic
taste enjoys this—it had yet a sound substance of truth
underneath its ornamentation. The bishop's fine presence
and dignified delivery added to the charm of his words.
Instinctively one thought of St. Columba; and wished that
the Irish Church of that time—Catholic, not Roman Catholic; nor Protestant, for there were as yet no corruptions
to protest against — could have remained as it then was,
one and indivisible; sanctifying and dignifying the secular
power as only a Church can which has in it the best of the
land.

It may seem a strange thing to say of a faith whose first
promulgators were a handful of fishermen—but I believe
no country ever prospers in which the ministers of religion
are principally drawn from its lower classes. The great
misfortune of Ireland is that many of its priests—Catholic
priests I mean—are taken from the peasantry, imperfectly
educated, and consequently narrow-minded. This should
not be in any Church. Let us give to God the best we
have: churches that will elevate men's minds to him
" who dwelleth not in temples made with hands;" and
clergy, who are men of education and refinement, not only
Christians but gentlemen—followers of Him whom an old
poet, Dekker, aptly calls,

" The first true gentleman that ever breathed."

August 30th.—We left Londonderry with regret—as, indeed, we had hitherto left every place—but for the inevitable necessity of pushing on.

THE GAP OF BARNES.
(From a Drawing by F. Noel Paton.)

And here I must pause to account for the fact that this town, where we found so much to interest us, goes unillustrated; and that of the illustrated places, Rathmullan, the Gap of Barnes, Muckish from Ards, and Horn Head, I can give no description at all. Author and artist, who had hitherto followed on one another's track, here found their ways divide. For pictorial purposes he avoided towns, and chose the beautiful country about Lough Swilly, which furnished endless subjects for the pencil. But, alas! there, as in many other parts of Ireland,

"All save the spirit of man is divine"

—the spirit which urges man to do his best to civilize himself and rise from the cave-dwellings of the original savage into the decent ways, the "sweetness and light," of an intelligent community.

"You cannot come here," wrote our artist; though he knew we did not mind roughing it, in moderation, and that our wants were of the simplest kind. "There is not an inn anywhere that a lady could stop at."

So all that splendid coast, made easily visitable from Derry by the little Buncrana railway, must remain unchronicled by me. How beautiful it is, was told us this morning by a gentleman whom we met accidentally in the coffee-room—an English landowner and M.P., travelling through all the worst parts of Ireland, in order to see with his own eyes the state of the country. Unlike many a politician, he felt it due to his constituents not to attempt to speak about what he did not understand. So he had spent his autumn holiday in wandering through the poorest, wildest, or most "congested" districts. It seems strange that in such a depopulated land there should be any congestion of population, yet so it is. In many places throughout Ireland the land cannot possibly sustain its children, and emigration — or eviction — becomes not a cruelty, but a necessity. If only the people could be planted out — like lettuce — over a larger surface in their own country, or given some industries that would maintain them independently of agriculture—often the hopeless tillage of an all but barren soil.

"Yet, one thing I am very clear of," said the M.P.

(after giving numerous details to prove his opinion)—" that this is a country of enormous possibilities most lamentably wasted. Who wastes them, or whose fault it is and has been that they are wasted, I will not undertake to say."

Nor will I, though I cordially agreed with the kindly-hearted Englishman, who had come to Ireland without a single Saxon prejudice, and was leaving it without an atom of Saxon animosity in his heart. Everywhere, he declared, he had been received, by the poorest and most wretched of the people, with civility and kindliness; and everywhere he had been struck not only by the misery, but by the dull indifference to it, and the want of any effort to avoid it.

" For instance," he said, " yesterday was as pleasant and restful a Sunday as ever I spent in my life. I put a book in my pocket, took the little railway to Fahan and Buncrana, and passed the day in wandering for miles along the grand sea-shore. The place I stopped to dine at looked well enough outside, and must originally have been a very good house; but the Atlantic storms had beaten it almost to pieces, and no one had ever attempted to repair it. Your Irishman can do wonderful things — why is it that he never can keep on doing them?"

Why, indeed? Perhaps, I might have said, because the volatile Celtic nature needs the Saxon phlegm to give it stability—even as absolutely pure gold can never be worked without a certain alloy of less valuable ore to harden it. But this would hardly have been civil to the excellent

Briton, who had come to Ireland with such good intentions.

"Now," he continued, dilating on the beauty of the whole of this quadrangular peninsula, bounded on two sides by the Atlantic, and on the two others by Lough Swilly and Lough Foyle, "if anywhere near the coast an enterprising speculator, English or Scottish, would start a good hotel, built ever so plainly, and fitted up ever so simply, provided it were comfortable—this would benefit the country more than all the harangues about 'driving the stranger out of the land.' Far wiser to bring him in, and his money with him. The way to civilize a country is to open it up to other countries. Neither families nor races are the better for isolation."

The honest M.P. was right. Surely, the cry of "Ireland for the Irish" is as unpatriotic as it is short-sighted and unwise. Only by immigration from other countries can baneful national characteristics be worn away, and national prejudices be smoothed down. A generous "give and take," I agreed, is invaluable for the civilization of the world.

"Then," he said, "instead of Ireland hating England and England bearing on her contemptuous face the warning 'No Irish need apply,' you would mix up the two countries as much as possible, in things commercial, political, intellectual, and social?"

"Certainly—especially the latter. I think, as was discovered often in ancient times, Celt, Scot, and Saxon might do a much better thing than exterminate their enemies—marry them!"

At which truly feminine solution of the Irish difficulty we all laughed—and parted.

Between Derry and Letterkenny is an innocent little railway, which seems to run chiefly for its own amusement, independent of passengers and time-tables. We had no difficulty in securing the carriage "all to ourselves," which the Barbarous Scot—who, like most of his countrymen, is not gregarious, and presupposes every unknown fellow-passenger to be a foe rather than a friend—considers a *sine quâ non* in railway travelling. So, congratulating ourselves on the absence of our fellow-creatures—alas! there were only too few to be got rid of in this thinly-populated land—we merrily began our day's journey, wondering much how it would end. For Letterkenny is the last point of steam communication in this desolate County Donegal. Henceforward we must trust to mail-cars—and any one who ever saw an Irish mail-car will understand what that means—or to private cars, which are not much better.

Still, "where there's a will there's a way." We had begun our journey, and meant to go through with it. Our artist's kindly warning had not included Letterkenny, and if it had, we were merely passing through. But we took the precaution of securing a carriage, and a dinner, at the one inn which, we were told, the little town possessed, kept by "the two Miss Hegartys."

During a long and not over-interesting journey, with pleasant glimpses of the shining lough on one side, and on the other very unpleasant wafts of flax-steeping—I think half-decayed flax has the most abominable smell to an English nose—we amused ourselves in speculating as to what the Miss Hegartys would be like, what sort of dinner they would provide for us, how quickly we could eat it and start off again.

"Half an hour," said the masculine ruler of our travelling destinies—"half an hour will be quite long enough to stay at Letterkenny."

In which we all agreed—and therein made a mistake, one of the not many mistakes of our tour.

Arrived at the terminus, after having stopped at every station since Londonderry while the officials of our train held interesting—and lengthy—colloquies with the country-folk, and then, as if taking a sudden thought, started us off again—we found waiting, not the aboriginal outside car, but a comfortable wagonet, which set us down in front of an inn, where, instead of a half-hour, we could well have stayed for a week. Dainty bedrooms, scrupulously clean, and actually pretty, with their neat lace and muslin furnishing; a sitting-room that had even a touch of the artistic about it; a dinner "fit for a king," and served punctually to the minute, and a Miss Hegarty—one of the two, who was the very opposite of the typical Irish landlady—we got all this for charges so small that they would be impossible except in a district where, as I had heard, you can get fowls for a shilling a piece, and the best of butter for ninepence a pound.

Yes, it was a mistake. We might, with the utmost comfort, have settled ourselves down here, and made excursions to Rathmullen, Rathmelton, Horn Head, Buncrana,

RATHMULLEN.
(*From a Drawing by* F. NOEL PATON.)

nay, even have gone back and examined Grainan Aileach. But in travelling, as in life, one discovers so many things done or left undone — afterwards! The only right thing is not to mourn over them, but try to amend them—next time.

We could not amend this error, for our rooms were taken at Gweedore—we must go on. So we ate our dinner, looked out from our window at what we heard was the Roman Catholic Bishop of Raphoe, said to be a cultivated and highly intelligent man; then watched the horses put

9

to the wagonet, and our luggage tied upon a supplementary
car, in the ingenious way that Irish cleverness does tie it,
and sits upon the top of it, as we saw an old man sitting,
as lightly as if he had been a large blue-bottle fly. He
drove away, with all our *impedimenta*—we earnestly hoping
not to find some of them lying .in the road; and shortly
afterwards we started for our thirty-mile drive—thirty Irish
miles—across one of the strangest, grandest, and most desolate regions that can be found in the United — yes, and it
should be united—Kingdom.

At first it was a slow, steady climb up a steep road,
with a wide stretch of cultivated land below, and in the
distance a range of mountains, one of them of rather peculiar shape, long and flat—"Muckish," briefly explained the
driver, and relapsed into silence. We thought to win him
by noticing his horses, at the sight of which any English
coachman, accustomed to sleek steeds and trim harness,
would have stood aghast.

 · "They will be pretty well tired by the time they reach
Gweedore, I fear!" (Nobody liked to suggest that they
might never reach it at all.) "Are they accustomed to the
journey?"

Jehu nodded.

"But, of course, you will let them rest the night there?"

An expressive gesture of distaste, which we did not
understand then—we did afterwards. "They'll be back at
Letterkenny to-morrow morning."

There was no more to be got out of him, so we left him
to his duties, and prepared ourselves for one of those drives

to which travellers in Donegal must get accustomed, wondering which is most interminable, the length of the road, the patience of the driver, or the strength and endurance of these thin, wiry, hungry-looking horses—Irish horses, that will do forty miles as easily as fat English horses will do fourteen. Still, to pity them was useless; and their driver was very good to them, urging them more by voice than whip, and letting them go at a snail's pace whenever the road required it.

He was a dark, strong-featured, handsome fellow, with a firm-set, rather saturnine face, not at all like the lively Paddy of the south. Nor was he in the customary contented rags: his rough overcoat, whatever it covered, looked decent and whole. He took no notice of us or of our talking and laughter—which was considerable, for in the bright sunshine and keen mountain air our spirits rose amazingly—but sat on his box, unsympathetic, silent, and grim.

"Perhaps he is a Home-Ruler," suggested the Violet, who had all along expressed the greatest desire to see that awful specimen of an Irishman, to the English mind something equivalent to the mysterious gentleman with horns and a tail.

"He may have been evicted," added the Bird, who had the very vaguest notions of what eviction meant.

"Probably neither," said the Barbarous Scot, who always takes an eminently practical view of things; "he is just minding his horses, which is the best thing he can do."

But I had studied the human face too many years not

to be struck, even touched, by this one. There was in it a kind of set endurance, which was neither sullenness nor stupidity. And for a driver, an Irish driver, to go on for miles without a word, except to his horses, was a thing so uncommon that, as soon as the rest of the party descended and were safely disposed of for a long hill, I spoke to him.

He was civil, but no more. All attempts to get him into conversation failed. Still, I did not despair. The grand keynote to the Irish nature — will rulers ever find it out, and strike it ?—is sympathy.

Soon, we came upon a really pretty village, with a modern church, and an old ruin beside it.

" What is that ?"

" Kilmacrenan," he answered, and vouchsafed no more. We remembered that a clergyman, at breakfast that morning, had told us that we ought specially to notice the place, because a relation of his had lived there many years, and had had the honor of receiving in his vicarage Bishop Wilberforce, who declared afterwards

KILMACRENAN.
(From a Drawing by F. Noel Paton.*)*

that he "had never been happier in his life than at Kilmacrenan."

We should have dearly liked to test this possibility, to investigate the abbey, and learn something about it; but, as it was, we were obliged to content ourselves with that valuable episcopal reminiscence, and the sight of the pretty little vicarage, where a group of young people were playing lawn-tennis, which looked odd enough in this out-of-the-world nook, the last vestige of civilization that we came upon.

No one who has not seen them can imagine the intense desolation of these Donegal moors. You drive miles and miles without seeing a human being, or a sign of the habitation of one, nay, not even a beast or a bird, wild or tame. There are no trees to rustle, no rivulets to sing. Now and then comes a little lake, or rather an accumulation of stagnant bog-water; but of the noise of leaves or streams, so cheerful in solitary places, there is nothing—only silence, dead silence. On a sunshiny day this is dreary, but on a gray or wet day desolate beyond conception. Moorland and bog, bog and moorland, stretch on in level succession, so that you can often trace the road before you for miles; while the distant mountains, with lesser hills between, are continually changing their shape, as you change your route, and yet always distinguishable — Muckish, with its long "pig's back," and Erigal, conical and dazzling white. Such was the region we were passing through, varied, in a sense, and yet keeping, mile after mile, a strangely solemn monotony.
9*

At last a thought struck me, and I risked a question of our driver, whom the rest of the party had given up as hopelessly dour.

"Did Miss Hegarty explain to you that we wanted to turn off a little from the main road to see Dooan Well?"

"Is it the holy well of Dooan ye mane, ma'am? It's nothing to see—ye'll not care for it."

I thought differently. Our artist had written that I should on no account miss seeing it—a tiny well, scooped out under a stone, to which good Catholics brought their sick to drink, pray, and be healed. The utter desolation of the place, in the midst of a wild moorland, miles and miles away from any town or village—the absorbed devotion of the pilgrims, who had come hither from great distances, had struck not only himself but an English clergyman who was with him, as a remarkable phase of humanity. And as my business was to see not only nature, but human nature, I was determined to go.

Not altogether unopposed. "It's two miles at least out of our way!" "Nobody ever heard of the place!" "All a humbug from beginning to end"—were reasons successively urged—and combated. Finally, our driver, who had looked as if he did not hear us, but probably did listen all the time, was told to drive to Dooan Well.

We left the good main road—the Donegal roads, if long, are exceedingly good—and plunged into a narrow track, that melted gradually into no track at all. The bare moorland stretched out on all sides as far as we could see. Nothing else. Not a man, nor a beast, nor a cabin, was visible.

HOLY WELL AT DOOAN.
(From a Drawing by F. Noel Paton.)

"I don't believe there's any well at all," said the most incredulous of us.

Whether or not the driver heard I cannot tell, but he pointed a little ahead to a group of people just dismounting from a cart — one of those rough, jolting machines which are the only means of locomotion for the poor in Ireland, and compared to which an outside car is luxurious.

"There's the well; ye'd better get down."

He stopped his horses determinedly—I think he crossed himself, but am not sure. At all events, he seemed resolved to keep—and that we should keep—at a respectful distance from the holy well.

Whatever the rest thought—and I asked them no questions, for each must judge for himself, and feel for himself—to me there was something infinitely touching in the sight. A tiny spring, half hidden by a big stone; near it a little forest of walking-sticks, each with a rag tied on the top—votive offerings or mementoes of those who went away cured; and in front of it a small group. When our artist came the pilgrims were women, but to-day they were all men. Four laborers, in the prime of life, but weak and wasted, and each with that most pathetic thing to see in a working man—clean, smooth, white hands—crept feebly from the cart to the well. One after the other each knelt down before it, his head level with the water, and drank, two or three times, praying between whiles with the dumb earnestness of desperate faith.

Two or three women stood at a little distance watching them, in absolute silence, a rare thing for the lower-class Irishwomen, and with faces that one felt it was an intrusion to look at. They took no notice of us whatever, nor did the sick men. All seemed entirely absorbed in their devotions, and in the errand which had brought them hither. Our party, whatever they thought, had the grace also to maintain a respectful silence, and shortly to move on towards a little hill, or rather a huge rock gradually covered with vegetation, in the shelter of which was one small cabin, no other house being near. Then, having seen enough, they started to walk ahead of the carriage across the moor, which lay quiet in the afternoon shadows of a perfect August day.

When they were safely disposed of, I came back to the well. The four men had never ceased praying. I touched the oldest and sickliest of them on the shoulder; he started, and looked up with an eager face, then down at the coin I put into his hand. He hesitated to take it.

"A Protestant lady gives you this, and hopes you will soon get well."

"Thank ye, missis. A blessin' on ye," was all he answered, and went back to his prayers.

The other three looked up for a minute, but said nothing; asked nothing; and kept on counting their beads and muttering as before. Neither the sick men nor their friends made the slightest attempt to beg charity, though they were evidently the poorest of the poor. And as I passed the cart which had brought them hither, the women who stood or sat beside it — or knelt, saying their beads, all equally silent and in earnest—scarcely cast a glance at me.

A little farther off, but equally unnoticed by them, was our carriage and its saturnine driver. As he helped me in, he looked keenly at me—and seeing that my face was as grave as his own, spoke.

"Ye found the holy well, ma'am?"

"Yes. Do many people go there?"

"Hundreds. I've seen the place black with people. They come from all parts of the country, and even from Australia."

"And they expect to go home cured?"

"They always are cured," was the decisive answer.

I did not contend the point, neither with him nor with

the sceptics whom I picked up presently, and who, *sotto voce*, out of tenderness to the man's feelings, began to argue the question. But there are things which cannot be argued, only felt.

"All humbug!" said the most incredulous. "These people saw we were coming, and knelt down on purpose, thinking we should give them something."

I suggested that they had taken no notice of us, and never asked us for a halfpenny

"Then it must be pure imagination—faith, or whatever you choose to call it."

"But what is imagination?" I said — "the intangible thing which produces such tangible results? And what is faith? which often cures better than all the doctors."

"Do you think these holy wells ever really cure people?" was asked by one of the English damsels of the Wild Irish Girl, as being more familiar with the subject than they.

"I know they do. There was a young woman in my district in Dublin who had a perfectly useless arm : the bone was diseased, the doctors said, and the case was incurable. She asked me if she should go, as her friends advised, to a holy well. All hope being at an end, I, though a good Protestant, of course said yes. She went, and returned cured—able to use her arm like other people. Now, what do you say to that?"

Why, we could say nothing. Even the incredulous Scot, fairly nonplussed, ceased arguing, and turned his attention to the seemingly endless moor, bare and bleak as

HORN HEAD.

(From a Drawing by F. NOEL PATON.)

ever, though softened into beauty by the fast-coming twilight. How in the world would those four sick men stand
being jolted back across it for miles and miles, in the darkness, and in that rough cart?

Yet, thinking of many people I know — clever people,
good people, who believe in nothing; to whom the vast
mechanism of the universe is mere mechanism, with no
guiding spirit behind it; who see only with the fleshly eye,
and admit only as much as the fleshly hand can handle, the
fleshly brain comprehend—it was almost a comfort to think
also of those poor souls, simply *believing*, even though their
belief may be no more than superstition. But it answers
its end. It teaches, as all the wisdom of the age likewise
teaches at last, that there is a limit to wisdom, a boundary
beyond which the keenest intellect cannot pass, when the
greatest sage must sit down beside the most ignorant
peasant, and say to himself practically the same words—
happy if he does say them and feel them!

> " I cannot understand—*I love.*"

Alas! both faith and love are sorely tried in travelling
through Donegal. The most earnest preacher of what is
called the "enthusiasm of humanity" would be hopelessly perplexed at sight of the small "holdings" which we
passed at rare intervals—a cabin little better than a pigsty, a bit of reclaimed land planted with potatoes, a peat-
stack cut from the nearest bog, sometimes a half-starved
cow not much bigger than a sheep, and a few fowls. As
for the human beings we saw, adults or children—they

looked like heaps of walking rags, surmounted by a wild
shock of dark hair, under which gleamed those wonderful
Irish eyes. How they managed to carry on existence, in
any form higher than that of a brute beast, seemed, to the
civilized eye, incomprehensible.

And yet Nature, in her terrible indifference, was so
grandly beautiful. Owencarrow river, Muckish, Carro-
trasma, and many other mountains, we passed, just catching the names, but finding it difficult to individualize anything. The impression left was of an interminable splendid sameness, which yet had an infinite variety. The air
was so invigorating, though soft, that the girls felt as if
they could walk on forever, and they did walk, out of
compassion to the horses, who toiled patiently on ; while
looking back—in that bare, flat moorland it was generally
visible for miles—we could see the car with our luggage,
and the old man sitting on the top, following patiently
after.

So we went on, till suddenly appeared a large lough,
ending in a lovely glen.

" What is that ?" I asked.

" Lough Veagh ; Glen Veagh."

" Mrs. Adair's place ? Is that the castle at the head
of the lough ?"

The driver nodded, looking darker and more " dour "
than ever. And this time I could guess why.

Some years ago, in Glen Veagh was enacted a tragedy,
which, though it has reached me with many variations, is,
I think, allowed by both sides to have its foundation in

certain facts, which, as near as I could get at them, were
these. A certain Mr. Adair, a wealthy Scotsman, bought
large tracts of land here, and had many contests with his
tenants, with whom he was far from popular : being an
absentee landlord, leaving his affairs to be administered
by his agents, who probably understood the peculiarities
of Irish nature as little as their master. One — no, more
than one of them — was murdered. Then Mr. Adair declared that, if in three months the murderers were not
given up, he would evict all the inhabitants of the glen.
Any person acquainted with Ireland can guess the result.
Everybody knew, but nobody told. Much exasperated,
Mr. Adair kept his word. The innocent suffered with the
guilty. Every family, women and children, young and
old, was turned out on the moor — for eviction here, in
this desolate place, means entire homelessness.

"And what became of them?" I asked, when the driver
and I were left alone in the carriage, and I had somehow
made him understand that I knew the story, and was
sorry for the poor souls — at least, for the old folks, the
women and children.

"Some died, ma'am, and some settled in other parts.
A good many went to America. Anyhow, there's not
one o' them left here. Not one."

"And Mr. Adair?"

"He's dead."

The man set his teeth together, and hardened his face
—a face I should not like to meet in a lonely road. It
was the first glimpse I had had, since our coming to Ire-

land, of that terrible blood - feud now existing between landlord and tenant, in which neither will see the other's rights — and wrongs; nor distinguish between the just and the unjust, the good and the bad.

"But Mrs. Adair is living still? and I was told yesterday that she was a kind woman, spending heaps of money upon the place, residing there herself? That will do good, surely?"

"Maybe."

"And she may understand the people better than her husband did. What is she like?"

The driver's countenance relaxed a little. "I've often druv her from Letterkenny. She's a sweet-spoken lady enough" (oh! if Irish land-owners did but understand the value of that "sweet speech"), "an' she likes the counthry—she comes here as often as she can."

"Nobody would harm *her*?"

"Sure, no, ma'am! But for Mr. Adair—he was a hard man. He's betther dead."

And then, as the rest of the party joined the carriage, my friend shut his mouth, and opened it no more.

"Is he a Home-Ruler?" whispered the Violet; "or a Fenian? or — whatever you call them?" The confused English mind takes in no political distinctions here.

I neither could nor would answer. But I think I could better understand the causes which work out such terrible results—the smouldering flame ready to blaze up the instant some incautious or malignant hand puts a torch to it. And this underground fire has been burning for cen-

turies. Oceans of extraneous "talkee-talkee" will never
put it out. Nothing, I believe, ever will, except the con-
tinuously just and righteous acts of the righteous inhabitants—and especially the land-owners—of Ireland.

But now the day was darkening fast, all the more for
one of those sudden mountain storms, that came up from
what seemed a long chain of loughs, with hills behind,
and hid both from us. The finest part of the journey,
where the road passes along Lough Dunlewy and Lough
Nacung, we therefore scarcely saw. But it was, we guessed,
like most mountain scenery, whereas that we had just
passed through was quite individual — like nowhere else.
And truth to tell, we were growing very tired, nor sorry
to exchange the picturesque for the practical. But our
troubles were only temporary—a few miles more and there
awaited us shelter, tea, and bed. It may have been weak,
but as I thought of all these comforts, I could not get
out of my head those poor souls turned out helpless on
the bleak hillside at Glen Veagh nearly twenty years
ago.

The storm lasted long enough to hide from us a good
deal — not everything. By and by Mount Erigal reap-
peared, dimly outlined, and a few stars of light — on the
earth, not the sky, showed we were at last coming within
reach of human habitation. Still, several miles had yet
to be traversed, with the long, narrow lough on one side,
the conical hill on the other. Not till it was nearly dark
did we stop suddenly at a group of trees, and drive under
a gateway into an enclosed courtyard — as I had remem-

10

bered driving, soaked to the skin and aching in every bone, one wet night exactly fifteen years before.

Gweedore Hotel. Two of us recollected it well, and were delighted to see it, again. The rest jumped down with eager curiosity, not a bit the worse for their day's travelling, and hastened to see after their luggage, which was close behind.

For a wonder, it was a strange hand which I felt helping me out of the carriage; and a voice, so kindly, even tender, that it quite startled me, said, as I descended,

"I'm afraid ye're very tired, ma'am. But ye'll get a good rest at Gweedore."

It was the (supposed) Home-Ruler.

PART V.

GWEEDORE.

GWEEDORE—or Guidore, as it is sometimes written and spoken, but in these old Irish names both spelling and pronunciation seem to be entirely a matter of taste —Gweedore is a place not unknown in England, especially to salmon-fishers. Nearly fifty years ago Lord George Hill, a landlord whose property lay in Derry, acquired in this desolate region a large tract of almost useless land, consisting principally of moorland and bog. He built there a small hotel—in a glen, pretty but not striking, watered by the Gweedore and Clady, two valuable salmon rivers—hoping to make it "a lodge in the vast wilderness," whither fishermen and tourists might resort, and gradually to gather round it a thriving village. For years he strove against countless difficulties, trying to reclaim the bog and turn it into cultivated land, which can only be done by long and patient manipulation; he started various industries, acquainted himself with the real condition of the people, educated and elevated them, and by every means which a good landlord has in his power tried to make "the desert blossom as the rose."

Of Lord George Hill and his work,—all ended now; he has been dead some years—I have heard, as one continually does hear in Ireland (and elsewhere also!), two diametrically opposite accounts. The one represents him as being like his neighbor, Mr. Adair, "a hard man," ready to grind the faces of the poor; or, at best, a man of good intentions and bad fulfilments, carrying out his will—or his crotchets—at all risks and costs. The other picture is of a kindly landlord, full of the enthusiasm of humanity; making mistakes sometimes, but earnestly trying to do all the good he could, in spite of being constantly thwarted, misunderstood, and misrepresented.

Between these two opposing characters, each vouched for with equal violence, history may choose. I myself prefer the latter, since it is generally safer to believe the best than the worst of anybody. And, besides, I have a vivid personal remembrance of the kind old man—his eager delight in his philanthropic hobbies; his love for his own country and people; the energy with which he used to drive, weekly, in all weathers, the weary miles between his own house near Letterkenny and the hotel at Gweedore, looking after its affairs to the minutest detail.

The building, quadrangular, and of two stories only, runs round three sides of an open courtyard, the fourth forming the stables and offices. Into this courtyard all doors enter, the windows being on the outside, an arrangement very desirable in this region of sea winds and mountain storms. The aspect is south and southwest, so that the range of small parlors below and small bedrooms above is always cheerful and bright. The one large apartment, used as a dining and coffee room, has a comfortable family look, with its long single table and its exclusively feminine attendants—the only man in the inside household being the necessary Boots.

We remembered it all—the pleasant little garden under the windows, the river beyond, into which dwindle Lough Luie and Lough Nacung, with the wide, open glen in the distance. Within, too, there was no change, except for the natural wear and tear of many years. The row of cosey parlors, each with its name above the door, and provided with arm-chair and sofa, was just as when Lord George so kindly welcomed us there, and talked to us all evening, with the eager enthusiasm of an earnest man, of all he had done and all he meant to do.

He is gone now, and his work, much criticised by his enemies and half forgotten by his friends, is all ended; but the hotel still holds its ground, the centre of an apparently thriving village, and of a little community concerning whom one who had spent half a lifetime among them said to me, "The Gweedore people are the best people possible, if only they were let alone." And those who know Ireland know what that means.

Well I recalled a dark, stormy night fifteen years ago, when, after five-and-thirty miles on an outside car, in pelting rain, we drove into this same quadrangle, soaked through and utterly exhausted, to hear the cruel answer, "You will have to go on to Bunbeg, we can't make room;" when a benevolent-looking old gentleman stepped forward, saying, " You *must* make room," and while an extemporized bedroom was got ready, took us into his own parlor, and warmed and fed us. It was Lord George Hill.

Ever since, Gweedore had been to us the ideal of what a tourists' hotel ought to be—especially in these wild regions, where even the necessaries of life are with difficulty obtained, and luxuries become impossible. Tourists who like luxury, and exist on outside show, must not go to Gweedore. Everything there is of the simplest and plainest kind, and yet of the very best.

Neither in this nor in any other room was there any æsthetic taste, but there was a great deal of comfort. Perfect was the cleanliness of the tiny bedrooms, each with its iron bedstead and its strips of carpet across the spotless floor, its plain deal washstand and chest of drawers, its tidy curtain, and—oh, rare luxury in Ireland!—blinds that act, windows that open, and doors that shut! Everything was planned so as to be readily washable and brushable, and that it was washed and brushed with rigorous exactitude a glance showed. How different from a late experience—I will not say where; when pursuing a handful of errant pennies under the bed—a very handsome bed for a hotel—I came upon a mountain of dust, which seemed to have been deliberately accumulated, not for weeks, but months. Sad testimony to that fatal habit—in England said to be " so Irish!"—of putting evil out of sight instead of sweeping it clean away.

But we were here to enjoy, not to moralize. And those

who know how much enjoyment in travel depends on little
things, on coming in hungry to a well-cooked meal, and
stretching one's tired limbs on a decent, comfortable bed,
getting all one reasonably wants, and being kept waiting
for nothing, will understand our appreciation of Gweedore.

"Yes, we try to do our best, and keep it up as in Lord
George's time," said the present manager, Mr. Robertson,
and his pleasant and capable sister. "But it isn't as when
he was coming himself every week and taking an interest
in everything about the place. Lady George comes now
and again, but Captain Hill lives at a distance, and, of
course, is seldom here. And we have had our difficulties. We were boycotted once, but not for long; the
people found they could not do without us, so they gave
it up."

I could well understand this. Mad as is the blood-feud
between Protestants and Catholics, landlord and tenant—
both sides often seeming to act the part of the typical
Irishman who was so bent on sawing off a bough that he
sat on the end of it and sawed it off, between himself and
the tree!—still, the insanest of its enemies must see that a
good hotel, planted in a wild region like Gweedore, might
be made a permanent centre of civilization—employing labor, buying up provisions, and being a constant source of
income to all the country-side.

"We try to make it so," said Mr. Robertson, "but it is
uphill work." And he gave us many details, useless to repeat, which made my heart feel sick and sore; as indeed it
often did, to hear from opposite sides the most contradic-

tory versions of the same fact—if a fact at all—and see
this lovely and lovable Ireland made into a battle-ground,
where every one was ready to fight tooth and nail, not so
much against actual evil, as against anything that differed
from his own peculiar notion of what was good.

It was such a fine morning that the others decided to go
a-fishing in Lough Nacung, in charge of Paddy, the hotel
fisherman. But I, who never could understand the pleasure intelligent human beings take in inveigling to its destruction one small trout, preferred a meditative saunter
along the banks of the lough, interchanging an occasional
word with the two or three country people I met, and enjoying to the full the exceeding peace of the place—the perfection of a place for those who are able to do nothing,
since there is actually nothing to be done.

Gweedore must have been, when first colonized by Lord
George Hill, a district as innocent of civilization as if it had
been one of our beyond-sea possessions. Of archæological
or historical interest it had none—at least, none that was
known. Nor was it specially picturesque. After Glen
Veagh the broad chain of loughs diminishes to a rather
commonplace river, and Gweedore Glen, though broad and
bright, has no remarkable features, except the one mountain, Erigal, which from its rounded shape and exceeding
whiteness is noticeable everywhere. Though the sea is
only four miles off, there is here no sign of it; and save at
the salmon-leap, the river flows placidly between reedy
banks, half moorland and half bog. In short, one can
hardly say what is the charm of Gweedore—and yet it has

GWEEDORE GLEN.
(*From a Drawing by* F. NOEL PATON.)

a charm, which we felt on the very first day, and never ceased to feel.

Perhaps it is the exceeding deliciousness of the air; fresh but soft, more like the air of Dartmoor than any place I know, and yet with all the bracing qualities of a mountain. Then the wide glen—open, not shut-in—is so dry and bright; every ray of sunshine being caught by and reflected from the glittering sides of Mount Erigal. On this last day of August it seemed to be full summer still; one of those calm, clear days which make one feel mere existence to be a blessing. A "quiet day" we had determined it should be—to lie upon our oars (which we did literally, most of us, for a good many hours, of which the re-

sult was a few, a very few, almost infantile trout, for breakfast next morning), to do nothing, think of nothing, in
short to be absolutely, ingloriously, or gloriously, idle.

For me, I was content merely to wander along the solitary road and watch white Erigal shining in the sun. Of
its geological formation I know nothing, but it is a rather
remarkable mountain to look at; on one side not difficult
to climb, but the other is a succession of smooth slopes,
down which apparently a single slide would take you to the
very bottom. You, or whatever might be left of you. One
shivered to think of it. And when, in the middle of dinner, two young tourists came in, and we guessed from their
talk that they had been over Mount Erigal, we regarded
them with curiosity.

They were English—apparently University men, and gentlemen—rather a contrast to the " commercial gentlemen "
species which we had encountered lately; two nice-looking
young fellows, brothers or friends, and ready to speak when
spoken to—for there was a kind of pleasant sociableness
about this Gweedore hotel, which, like many other Irish
hotels, had been nearly empty since the disturbances.

"Yes," one of them said, "we walked to-day about
seventeen miles, and then we climbed Mount Erigal. We
did well enough till we got to the top, and we had a fine
view; but then the mist came on, we lost the path, and descended on the wrong side, sliding pretty nearly the whole
way. We were not sorry to be safe at the bottom."

I should think not! How they ever got down alive was
a mystery to me, who had been watching the mountain all

MOUNT ERIGAL, GWEEDORE.
(*From a Drawing by* F. NOEL PATON.)

the afternoon. But they seemed to take it very coolly, and though they looked tired and battered, and disappeared early, had clearly enjoyed themselves—after the wholesome fashion of so many young Englishmen, who work their brains for nearly all the year, and then in their brief holiday work their bodies too, to the last limit of physical endurance, and find pleasure therein. Which it is—to simple honest natures. We all liked the lads, and finding they were quite ignorant of the neighborhood, took pains to explain to them what there was to see.

"We'll take a day's rest, I think," said the elder; "and then we go on to Carrick. We haven't any time to throw away."

No more had we. Who has, I wonder? So we all parted, having mapped out next day, which was to be a most interesting day for me, being the fulfilment of a purpose which I had wished to carry out for fifteen years.

"Fifteen years!" laughed my girls, to whom it seemed an eternity. But it is a standing joke that my plans always do come to pass, probably because I have an infinite patience in waiting for them.

September 1st.—"And a delightful day! Now we shall go and see Skull Island."

Which was the place I had told them of, and evoked in them nearly as great an interest as my own.

The case was this. On my first visit to Gweedore, wandering aimlessly about, we had gone to Bunbeg, a little fishing village about four miles off. There we visited a small island—at low water a peninsula—a mere sand-heap, lying in ridges that sloped landward towards the bay. In this sand-heap I found to my amazement a quantity of human bones—leg-bones, arm-bones, skulls—lying so close to the surface that with a stick or umbrella you could have digged them out of the sand by dozens.

I asked the man who had guided us across the sandy causeway—for it was low water—if I might take one as a curiosity.

"'Deed, ma'am, and ye may take as many of them as ye like. We lets the children have them to play with. There's heaps of them about here. That's why it's called Skull Island."

SKULL ISLAND.
(From a Drawing by F. Noel Paton.)

But to any further inquiries he only shook his head. He knew nothing—nobody knew nothing. He supposed they were "just bones." He seemed, indeed, hardly to take in the fact that they were human bones like himself. As to how they got there, he was in a state of entire ignorance—and indifference. Whether the island, considered a sacred spot, as all islands were in what we call the "dark" ages, had been used as a burial-place—whether it was the scene of a great battle or a shipwreck, and this idea seems possible—since, the guide told me, most of the skulls found had such splendid teeth, and therefore must have been those of young men—all these matters of intense interest were to that worthy man nothing at all. He and every other person I spoke to on the subject persisted that nobody knew anything—and certainly nobody cared—about Skull Island.

So, routing among the sand, which was spread so lightly that at the depth of six inches I might easily have disinterred any quantity of bones, I picked up two "beautiful" skulls, quite perfect, the teeth being white, strong, and regular,—such as one rarely sees even in a young person in these degenerate days. I wrapped them up in my shawl and carried them down to the boat, which was waiting to take us across what had an hour or two ago been a firm pathway of sand.

"You're never going to take those things home?" said my companion, in much disgust, sitting down by mistake upon one of them. But I saved the other, and, hiding it in my bonnet-box, brought it safe to London and gave it to a learned friend; who admired it exceedingly, said the teeth were very remarkable, and the cranium also; being of a peculiar shape, unknown among our modern races. Of its age, or how long it had been buried, he could offer no conjecture whatever.

This deepened the mystery. For years Skull Island positively haunted me. I spoke of it to many archæological friends; several promised to investigate it. But the great distance and the utter absence of all historical or traditional data always stood in the way. At last I determined to go myself, and, after the usual amount of years of waiting, here I was!

The Barbarous Scot, who is not archæological, and openly expresses his dislike to "dead men's bones," viewed my excitement with a tender pity, but helped me to indulge in it by securing a car at the earliest possible hour after breakfast. The girls were interested too—especially the Violet, who seemed to think the skeleton of a defunct Norseman might be almost as curious a sight as a live Home-Ruler. So off we started, in the best of spirits, to see what we should see.

Bunbeg is an uninteresting place in itself, but it is the grand emporium of commerce of the district, and, for Gweedore, the nearest point of contact with the external world. The only other means of traffic is by horse and car along the mountain roads. When, some little time ago, the owner of the extensive salmon fisheries here was boycotted, and warned that his fish would be stopped in their transit across country, he, with true English coolness, arranged that the Sligo and Derry boats should call at Bunbeg. This sea-traffic has resulted in bringing most of the necessary provisions to be got in towns by that route. Consequently the keeper of the Bunbeg store is a very useful and important person in the neighborhood.

We lounged about his place—amusing ourselves with the usual heterogeneous collection of goods that one finds in a country shop; and looking at the tiny harbor with its half a dozen idlers, who seemed to have nothing to do but contemplate that novel sight—ourselves. Apparently the only interesting place near was Gweedore Catholic Chapel, on the opposite side, where we had noticed the road divide. It is built in a ravine, down which not many years ago there suddenly came pouring a waterspout from the mountains. It broke, and the chapel was washed away, an old woman who happened to be in it at the time being drowned. The exertions of the energetic parish priest rebuilt it better than before, but, with the fatal persistency of a half-civilized people, who will not profit by experience, it was built in the very same place; so that the next cyclone may, in that narrow ravine, wash it away altogether —which probably the Protestant Church, seated on a hill above Bunbeg, would consider "a judgment."

Alas! to strangers those feuds, religious and political, which in secluded districts take such huge proportions, dwindle to nothing, only provoke a smile—or a sigh. Was there the same kind of thing—petty strifes, petty jealousies —furious loves, and unreasoning hates—among those poor bones that we were going to search for in the sand of Skull Island?

We began to question whether we should ever get there. No boat or boatman could be found, and the tide was fast receding.

"Ye'll be able to cross on foot soon," said a very respectable-looking man, who had taken a kindly interest in our proceedings. "I'll guide ye, and keep ye safe out of the quicksands. I've nothing better to do"—seeing we hesitated — "I'll take ye there and bring ye back. It's no throuble."

So he marched on ahead of us for what seemed nearly a mile's walk, up hill and down dale, and then across a bit of boggy ground which sloped down to the sea-shore. There, just at the entrance of the harbor, across a stretch of wet, shiny sand, with tiny rivers of sea-water flowing through it, was the little sand-island, wholly bare of vegetation, sloping upward, ledge after ledge, to the high boulders which formed its rock-boundary on the seaward side.

"That's it—that's Skull Island," said our unknown friend, who was grave and taciturn, but still had more than once held out a civil and most welcome hand to help us through the rough walking. "Ye can easily cross to it now—I'll show ye the way."

And following him in the driest places we could find, with occasional jumps over the shining channels of water that intersected the never too solid sand—we reached the spot. I well remembered it of old—the strange, lonely burial-place of those unknown, long-forgotten dead.

"Yes—that's the ridge where the bones mostly lie. Lord George Hill, just before he died, made me bury a lot o' them, but ye'll find plenty yet. Every strong wind blows the sand away—and they turns up again. It's a quare place to have chosen for a burying-ground."

We agreed. But on questioning him we found—though he had lived at Bunbeg nearly all his life—that the good man knew no more about Skull Island than we did. Whether there had been a battle there, or a shipwreck—and the fact that most of the skulls had their teeth very perfect seemed to imply that the mass of dead were chiefly young men—or whether it was the ordinary burial-place of some of the many forgotten monasteries, planted everywhere by the old Irish "saints" in their system of ecclesi-

11

astical polity, which was so strangely, completely civilized, amid the barbarism of neighboring lands — all was the merest conjecture. There the bones were; and nothing more could be discovered concerning them.

We set to work hunting, and in two or three minutes had found an arm-bone, a leg-bone, two bits of jaw-bone with exceedingly fine teeth, and several finger-bones, all bleached white, and of that rare perfection of shape and fitness which sometimes startles us living beings to think how "fearfully and wonderfully made" is the framework we carry about with us, the temporary mortal residence of this immortal "I." And then, hidden under a ledge of soft sand, we came upon a good many more.

By and by, two black figures were seen crossing the sands—our young friends of the evening before, to whom I had explained about Skull Island. We asked them to join in the work, which they did *con amore.*

A curious scene it was—that sunshiny spot, so quiet and silent, except for the sound of the Atlantic waves breaking against the rocks at the back—and those five young people on their hands and knees, digging eagerly with sticks, umbrellas, and fingers, for this unknown relic of an era utterly unchronicled. Soon they found it, the entire skeleton of a man — buried face upward in the sand. First was uncovered an arm-bone, then a leg-bone, both lying straight in their places; then the collar-bones, then a line of little bones forming the vertebræ. There he lay, except for the skull, which was missing—"streekit smooth," just as when he had been buried.

We might have wholly disinterred him; our guide, a little distance off, looking gravely on, neither helping nor hindering—but a sudden feeling seemed to come over us of the ghoul-like nature of our proceedings. The contrast between this gay, open-air company, with its youthful jests and laughter, and those poor bones, once as living as ourselves, struck us as something incongruous — even ghastly. The mirthful excitement ceased—one by one the young people stopped digging.

"I wonder what he was like when alive. Tall, probably—a Norse chieftain or a Viking."

"Or one of St. Columba's monks. Or, perhaps, a ship-wrecked sailor out of the Spanish Armada."

"Suppose we cover him up again," suggested some one —I think it was the Brown Bird, who has in her much of the tender spirit attributed to the robins in the "Children of the Wood." "What good will it do to dig him up? Let him rest."

All agreed. Silently and gravely the bones — or as many as had been removed—were put back into their places, under the overhanging ledge, and the sand piled carefully over them, so as to hide from less reverent eyes all vestiges of what was once a man. Only the finger-bone and two bits of jaw-bone, which I had put in my pocket, I found there a day or two afterwards, too late to restore—and so brought them home in safe seclusion among my lace caps.

Our quest ended, we sat and ate our lunch under shelter of one of the two or three boulders which marked the highest point of the tiny island, and whence we could see other islands a little farther out—Gola, Umphin, Inishfree, Owey. We wandered about the narrow limits of this one, and talked to our guide about it; but could get no information. He said we had been lucky in finding "a whole person," as that was not often found now—the children throw the bones about so much. Sometimes they picked up in the sand "curiosities," such as long pins of some metal—but nobody cared to preserve them. Nobody wanted old things hereabouts. There was a sunken ship lying out there (he pointed across the sea to a spot about three miles off). People said it was one of the Spanish Armada. At low water it was seen so clearly that you could almost have stood on the hull.

"And did no diver go down to see it?"

"Sure nobody would take the trouble," was the answer, with an indifferent smile. "About twenty-five years ago some gentlemen subscribed for the getting-up of an anchor —I saw it pulled out of the water—it was all rusty and covered with shells, and they sent it to a museum in Dublin."

We listened—some eagerly, some sceptically—but with all our cross-questionings the man kept to the same story, that the ship still lay there; many a boatman had sailed over it, and as for the anchor, he had seen it himself with his own eyes.

Good sea-eyes they were; for, looking across the Atlantic, he suddenly warned us there was a storm coming.

"Ye'd better get ashore afore it's on ye. Keep close afther me—there's quicksands here and there."

And with a care quite fatherly, he piloted us back the way we came—across the sandy causeway, not shiny now, but dull and ugly-looking, as if it could swallow us up if it chose. Was it by this road that the bodies were carried for burial—if indeed Skull Island had been a Christian resting-place in monkish times? However, conjecture was useless. Nothing could be found out, and probably nothing ever will be.

In parting from our guide, who had taken so much kindly trouble over us, he was of course offered some return. He put back the coin with a dignified independence.

"Thank ye, sir; but I couldn't take it. I'm not needing money. If ye'll come to my little place the lady can rest, and my sister will give ye all a cup of tea."

This was indeed unexpected, and though we wanted no tea, for it was only three o'clock, we could not refuse such kindly hospitality. So I walked on with our unknown friend, to whom we were equally unknown, as sociably as if we were Arabs meeting in the desert. On the way he told me, as many a stranger has done before, in words few and simple, but which touched me to the heart, a whole life-story. I shall not repeat it here, but I shall long remember it—and him.

The cottage, the sister, who had charge of the widower's children, and the children themselves, all interested me much; and the glass of milk with which I compounded for the tea, was perfectly delicious. On our departure our host shook hands with all of us, looking almost regretfully after his still unknown guests.

It was well he did. Not two minutes afterwards, by some queer equine manœuvre—there's no understanding your tricksy four-footed animals!—we felt the wagonet backing against a stone wall, with—as well as I can remember—a deep ditch below. The Brown Bird and the Barbarous Scot, who knew most about it, looked anxiously at one another; the rest of us sat dead silent, awaiting what might happen. And there is no saying what might have happened, had not our good friend darted forward, seized the horses' heads, and guided them into safety. We bade him a second and most grateful good-bye, feeling that we probably owed him our lives.

We were rather quiet all the way to Gweedore, and then our spirits rose. Either the Atlantic storm never came, or we had driven out of its reach—the afternoon was beautiful. All who could walk proposed to start off along the moorland road towards Falcarragh; I following after, in the leisurely way out of which old folks, who have courage to accept the fact that they cannot do like the young, may get so much pleasure, and trouble nobody.

It was a very lonely road, and yet so sweet; with the shining line of lakes stretching all the way to Glen Veagh, the smooth sides of glittering Erigal, on the left hand, the long thread of mountain road visible for miles, and the fresh, pure air, half mountain, half bog; one has to go to Ireland to learn the wonderfully bracing properties of bog air, the same above the surface as its preservative qualities below. Walking became a pleasure instead of a weariness. For an hour I met not a creature, except a big cart-horse carrying a young man and woman, without a saddle. Her scarlet plaid was over her head, with its neatly-combed, glossy black hair, her bare feet dangled, and her arms were round the young man's waist. They might have been sweethearts, but looked more like brother and sister, jogging along so steady and so grave.

I sat on the low turf wall and watched them, thinking what a picture they made, and wondering, as one does wonder sometimes, how life goes on among people different to ourselves in habits and education; what they think of, what they talk about, and how difficult it is to judge of their feelings by our own. And yet one ought to try to understand and get near them, as I tried, by smiles and biscuits combined, to win some little ragamuffins who were playing near two or three roadside cabins. One could scarcely tell whether they were boys or girls, their few clothes were so oddly heterogeneous. They hardly understood English, I thought, from the few words I got out of the biggest of them, but I managed to discover that they had seen a gentleman and three ladies walking up the road.

"If you see them again, go and speak to them, and say mother has gone home. Remember the words, mother —has—gone—home."

The small individual—I think the bundle of rags contained a boy—nodded solemnly, and passed my last biscuit over to two lesser infants, who regarded it as if they had never seen such a thing before, and never attempted to

cat it. Exceedingly doubtful as to how far I had been
understood—though I afterwards found my message had
been accurately and literally delivered—I spoke to a
woman whom I met shortly after and found that she
had seen my party.

"Three young ladies and a gentleman. That's yer husband, maybe? He's pretty well on"—in years, I suppose
she meant—"like yerself."

And she eyed me over, especially my stick, with simple
kindliness,' and slackened her brisk' pace to keep beside
me. She was a big, strong, middle-aged woman, in the
usual frieze petticoat and bright-colored shawl, with bare
head and feet. But her clothes were whole, her face was
clean, and her hair tidy. She carried a large bundle, and
was evidently bound for a journey of a good many miles.
We went on together, I putting my best foot forwards,
but in vain.

"I'm going too fast for ye, ma'am. Ye see, I'm used
to walking. An' my brogues"—glancing with sly humor
at her bare feet—"my brogues don't wear out."

I laughed, confessed my inferiority, and then we fell
into a long talk. She spoke slowly and a little disjoint-
edly, as if she had first to arrange her thoughts and
then translate them into a foreign tongue. I do not
attempt, never have attempted, to give the brogue; indeed,
here I rarely found it. The "stage" Irish, the unc-
tuous Cork and Limerick accent, and the Dublin twang,
are not noticeable in Antrim, Derry, and Donegal, where
the original Gaelic has been gradually changed into the

English taught at National Schools. Many of the older generation speak only Irish, but the younger population know both languages, though, as with this woman, their English comes to them like a foreign tongue—slowly, but correctly.

We talked a good deal about the state of the country. " It's been hard times with us for a long time," she said, " but things are mending a bit. Many of us have gone to America—there's no starving there. A kind English lady has been helping us in Donegal—the women, I mean —giving us work and paying for it. Maybe ye'll know her ?"

" Mrs. Ernest Hart," I suggested—glad to own that I did know her.

" Sure, that's the name. I don't work for her myself, but I know them as does. She pays them regularly, ye see. She's brought a little money into the country, and it's money we want; we're all so poor."

Yet the woman never asked, or by her manner hinted in the smallest degree, that *I* should give her money. Nor did I—her air of sturdy independence would have made me ashamed to offer it.

She gave me, in her unconscious candor, much information about Donegal, and asked of me no end of questions, after the simple fashion of country people, who take as much interest in you as they expect you to take in them; a refreshing change from the bitterly-learned reticence—or indifference—of towns. And when I said I would not hinder her longer, as I could not walk as fast as she could, she regarded me with a tender pity that was amusing.

"I see ye can't. Ye're not as young as ye have been, though ye're wearin' pretty well. Ye'd betther sit down a bit."

Which I did, on a tempting bank of turf; and watched her down the road, with her free, springy step, and upright carriage, fit to be mother to half a dozen Donegal "boys" —as no doubt she was. And I thought what splendid stuff these Irish peasants are made of, if only—to repeat what more than one compatriot said of them—"if only they were let alone."

Not let alone in neglect; that is a totally different thing. And yet there are difficulties—incomprehensible in England, where between the squire and his farm-laborer is a smooth succession of several ranks, each melting into the other, and continually meeting on mutual ground of help and kindliness. Education, too, is there a not impossible breaker of barriers. Sometimes the laborer's daughter becomes nurse or lady's maid at the hall, and the blacksmith's clever son has ere now been helped to school and college by the squire; and even come to sit at the squire's table. But such things are impossible, or held to be impossible, in Ireland. What bond of union could there be, for instance, between this poor woman I met and Mrs. Adair of Glen Veagh, with her five hundred miles of deer-park palings, and her twenty thousand pounds spent in improvements at the castle? Did they meet—which they are never likely to do—they

would regard one another, and judge one another, like
two beings out of different spheres, who scarcely owned
a common humanity.

The gulf between upper and lower classes—of middle
class there is almost none—is in Ireland enormous. The
lower class can never bridge it. Will the upper class
cross it to them? And how?—God only knows. Certainly demagogues do *not* know. Nor do many of the
" gentry " of the last generation—who preserve the fatal
traditions of the French aristocracy before the Revolution, and scarcely feel as if the common people were of
the same flesh and blood as themselves. The only hope
seems to be in the uprising of a new generation, with
wider eyes and calmer judgment, who can hold out a
helping hand to either side, teaching the one that

" The old order changeth, giving place to the new,"

and preaching to the other that justice between man and
man is due as much to the higher as to the lower stratum of society, and that the best of self-government
consists in ruling one's self. There may then be some
hope of Ireland's gaining that true freedom which is
only attainable by a prudent, peaceful, and law-abiding
race.

September 2.—A day of exclusively private life. Being
such, I long considered whether I should not pass it
over entirely. And yet this would be so great a *suppres-
sio veri*, that I have decided on the contrary. I shall give

no names, but the facts only; which are, many of them, already public property.

There are landlords and landlords. No doubt Ireland has suffered cruelly from the worst type of that order, who, generation after generation, lived recklessly, ruinously, in their Castle Rackrents, till their impoverished descendants of to-day, with the same extravagant tastes, the same contemptible pride, ashamed of economy though not of debt, have found it impossible to maintain "the family" in the only style which they consider its due. They therefore run away from what they dare not face; become permanent absentees, and spend in England or abroad the money they get out of the estate; keeping up the credit of owning property, but shirking alike its duties and responsibilities. Such landlords—and the Encumbered Estates Court has long proved how many there are—spendthrift "gentlemen," who have over-built, over-eaten, over-drunk themselves, and then racked their tenants to supply their own extravagances, have been the curse of Ireland. They deserve no mercy, only strict justice.

But there is another class who deserve justice also, and do not always get it, being included in the common howl against "landlordism," which is now sowing in Ireland all the seeds of civil war—I mean the "good old Irish gentleman" who has lived on his estate, as his fathers lived before him, spent all his money there, done his best for his tenants, exacted from them no more than his due, and shown an example of thrift, industry, kindliness, and charity, which if they did not imitate, it was their fault, not

his. Such landlords do exist; but with the usual pas-
sionate impulsiveness of the Celtic race, they are over-
looked—even as the cool-headed but prejudiced Saxon
overlooks the fact that every tenant in Ireland does not
go about armed with a gun, and, generally speaking,
has not the slightest wish to shoot his landlord, unless
coerced into so doing.

The landlord with whom we spent this day would
have smiled at any such idea! The instant we entered
his gates, after a drive of many miles over moor and bog,
we saw that it was not a Castle Rackrent. Nor, indeed,
a castle at all, but a comfortable modern house, led to
by a neatly-kept drive, through a wood where the large
primrose leaves showed what a blaze of yellow must be
there in spring. Across the lawn the ivy-covered ruins of
the ancient house implied a family home of generations,
as it had been, ever since the days of Charles I.; the
present owner, who came early into his property, having
lived on it, man and boy, for nearly seventy years.

He was really a picture, as he came out to welcome
us at his own door. Tall, white-haired, with a fine,
benevolent face, and the stately manner of the old school
of Irish gentlemen, which, alas! sometimes covers much
unworthiness, but when, as now, allied to intrinsic worth,
is, I think, unapproachable in its charm. His sons, two
out in the world and one with him here, were not unlike
him; and his daughter and daughter-in-law were of the
best type of kindly, cultivated gentlewomen common to
all countries.

Here, year after year, generation after generation, the family has lived, as all such families might do, and ought to do; making in this distant spot a centre of civilization, from which to radiate benefits, mental, moral, and physical—like the "little candle" of Shakespeare, which "throws its beams" so far: becoming, as every great house ought to be, a light to all the neighborhood round. Which, I have every reason to believe, is the case here; though of this landlord, as of many others, there have been bitter things said; for class-prejudice runs as rampant in the under as in the upper stratum of society—worse, perhaps, since narrow education breeds narrow judgment.

"My father has had a deal to go through," said to me one of the sons — he himself was silent. "Some of the allegations against him were so utterly untrue that I had to rise up and say so, for he never would have defended himself. It is astonishing how quietly he takes it."

"Why not?" said the old man with a good-humored smile. "I do my best for all my people. Yes, they certainly boycotted me, but as I had all 'within myself,' as the old woman said of her cocks and hens, pigs, and sheep, it didn't harm me much. Fuel was the chief difficulty. My poor fellows told me they dared not cut turf for me, but that I was welcome to help myself out of any of their stacks. However, I sent for fifty loads of coal from Derry, and got them landed on the beach close by; so we were warm and comfortable all the winter."

In this beach, which is most picturesque, lies imbedded,

they told us, under a great heap of drifted sand, the remains of one of the Spanish Armada — the third we had
heard of on this coast, at the Giant's Causeway, Bunbeg,
and here. I said this, suggesting that all the three had
originated in one, but it was not so. Our host's daughter
remembered, as a little girl, hearing of a great storm which
had swept away the sand and disclosed part of a brass
cannon. She begged her father to have it dug out, but
the next night the storm came on afresh, and drifted back
the sand, so that all trace of it was lost.

"But does nobody care to search for it?" I asked, as
often before, and received the usual reply.

"Oh, we are not archæological in Ireland. My father
has collected these"—showing me a cabinet full of ancient
rings and brooches, pins and bodkins, flint arrow - heads
and mediæval spurs. "They were all found on the beach
or in the bog."

"The bog we passed on our way, with great black
roots of trees sticking up every few yards?"

"The same. These are the remains of a primeval
forest, ages before it was converted into bog. But the
bog preserves everything. We found in it this, and this"
— showing me bronze ornaments and implements, of use
unknown. "My father has everything brought at once
to him, and he rewards the finder. No fear here of such
barbarisms as that of the gentleman who, picking up an
ancient gold ring, had it made into his bride's wedding-
ring, 'to save expense.'"

"Or," added some one, "the still more vandalish Gal-

way story, of the man who found in the bog what seemed
a circlet of old iron; his children broke it, and it was
yellow inside. So a pedler passing by bought it for a
pound. Some gentleman hearing this, went off to Dublin
after the pedler, but found it had just gone into the melt-
ing-pot. It was the crown of an old Irish king."

With such talk as this we whiled away the pleasant
afternoon, partly in the house and partly in the garden—
the old man's special delight. It was on the same pat-
tern as the Antrim gardens, and though so near the
sea, equally luxuriant. Thinking of the wretched " holdings " we had passed on the moor, it seemed a perfect
paradise.

"What a deal of labor you must employ here," I said;
" and what an advantage it must be to your small tenants
to earn a regular weekly wage as your under-gardeners
and such like, instead of starving on their acre, or half-
acre, of reclaimed bog land."

The master smiled rather mournfully. " They don't
think so. They would rather starve. It is not easy to
get them to work at anything regularly; they think they
are doing me a favor, and would prefer to dig their own
potatoes, and then idle away as they choose the rest of
their time. It looks more independent. You see the
Irish landlord has his difficulties—more than the English
landlord, a good deal. But we'll tide through. Perhaps
the next generation may succeed in teaching the Irish
peasant how to work—if our estates are not raffled away
from us by that time."

I had heard in Antrim of this raffling—indeed, I met a lady who had seen some of the tickets, sold for half a crown by some of the Nationalist leaders. In the grand uprising and demolition of property which they foretell, whoever owns a ticket with the name of an estate on it is to become the lucky possessor thereof! So much of an open secret is this that some of the landlords actually know the names of their would-be successors!

"Let us hope it will never come to pass," said this landlord, quietly. "Meantime I shall go on, as my fathers did before me, doing our very best for the place, and for my people, whether they understand it or not. My son, if he comes after me, will do the same."

Then we changed the subject, and stood admiring the fine sea-view, in which the principal object was Tory Island—much spoken of in newspapers some little time ago, as the scene of the sad wreck of the *Wasp.*

Tory Island is three miles long by half a mile broad. That it was long ago colonized and inhabited, is proved by the many remains of ancient buildings, churches, and crosses which lie half-buried in sand. There is also a curious Round Tower. Seaward, it opposes to the Atlantic a line of impregnable rocks, but landward it slopes down in green pastures. Its inhabitants are a curious race, half-fishermen, half-farmers, well-to-do and very independent. They are said to feed their cattle upon fish, and to tether their turbots by the tail in salt-water pools till the Derry and Sligo boats come to buy. Short as the passage is, sometimes the sea is so wild that for

12

weeks together the Tory-Islanders cannot cross to the
mainland; and in former times, before there was a chapel
or church there, eager lovers used, in bad weather, to resort to a novel way of getting married.   Two fires were
lit on the island and on the opposite shore—at one stood
the happy couple, at another the priest; when the fire
was put out, it was a signal that the ceremony was over
and the knot safely tied.

We were told also of wonderful sea-caves, so high that
boats can easily sail in or out of them; of McSwine's
Gun — a hole in a rock, through which the waves burst
with a loud report, and of a little hill or mound, in which
lies buried one Clogher Neilly, who murdered a "King of
Tory Island"—whosoever that notable monarch might be
—when he came to have his horse shod.   The said Neilly
was, I believe, hanged here, leaving behind him a prophecy
that while one stone of this mound remains, no other man
will ever be hanged in Donegal.   Let us hope it — unless
he deserves hanging.

It was a long drive back, with the sunset light shining
on the line of hills on our left hand; Muckish, with its
long "pig's back," from which it takes its name; Erigal
and Little Erigal, which look like mother and daughter,
being so similar in shape.   Nearing Gweedore, a mass of
black clouds rose up, making grand effects, but threatening one of those sudden deluges which make this climate
so interesting, and so inconvenient.

However, it came not.   We reached Gweedore un-
drenched, and found there our artist, who had arrived

in the mail-car from Falcarragh and Dunfanaghy—where
he had been obliged to rough it to an extent which he
assured us made the magnificent scenery round about unattainable to us womenkind. We had to content ourselves
with seeing what we could see in comfort. But we had
had another "white day"—and were thankful.

September 3d.—I think it rained all night—there are
seldom twenty-four hours in Ireland when it does *not*
rain; but the morning was lovely. While our artist went
sketching, we decided to go a-fishing up the chain of
lakes, at the head of which was the Marble Church—
built by a devoted Protestant, and to be consecrated in
a few days—and the Poison Glen; so called from its
total absence of vegetation, and, we were warned, the
perpetual presence of whole armies of midges.

Nevertheless we started courageously. The day was
hot and blindingly bright, and the fishes would not bite,
though six intelligent human beings devoted themselves
to their capture for eight mortal hours. One small trout,
about six inches long, was their only victim, and after
lying for half an hour in the bottom of the boat, it was
decided that being "young and foolish" he should be let
go. They resuscitated him in a pannikin, and then put
him back into the lough, when he feebly swam away—I
hope to give to his brethren a warning, for we never had
a bite afterwards.

But the fishermen—and fisherwomen—seemed to enjoy
themselves just the same. Mile after mile we floated over

the clear, shallow water — often so shallow that the boatmen had to step out into it, and fairly pull and push the
boat along. Getting wet seemed, this broiling hot day,
rather a treat than not. The fishers fished calmly on —
and the one who did not relish that occupation, and used
to sing a good deal in boats, years upon years ago, broke
out into "Gramachree Molly" and "The Pretty Girl Milk-
ing her Cow." At which the two Irishmen pricked up
their ears, remarking, politely, that "The ould folks did
betther nor the young sometimes," and hinting that Paddy
himself was "a fine singer intirely."

Of course we begged for Paddy's song, and listened
to it conscientiously for at least half an hour. It lasted
thus long, and was sung with a solemn countenance, in a
sustained minor monotone, interspersed by gutturals and
an occasional sound like a suppressed sneeze. We caught
no particular tune in it, but no doubt it had one — and
being in Irish, the words were a blank to us. Paddy
afterwards explained that they were about "a young
lady" whom a youth met "in the wilderness," married
and "tuk home," when his relations, considering the
family already too large, put her into a boat, rowed her
out to sea, and then and there "dhrownded" her. Poor
young lady!

His song done, Paddy joined his practical energies to
those of the gillie — who seemed as strong as Hercules —
in pulling the boat under a bridge, through the narrow
channel which divided the two loughs. Then we landed,
ate our lunch, and the rest went to see a chapel not far

off, while I distributed the remains of our food between
the two men and a third, a cripple with an extremely intelligent face, who joined us.

"He can't work," Paddy explained in a whisper; "so
he makes flies for the gentlefolks at the hotel. It's but
a poor living."

Nevertheless the man never begged, nor did they for
him. I heard the three talking and laughing together,
then the cripple left, and the other two men came up to
me to see if I was "comfortable." Somehow we fell into
a long talk—which I wish I could give, for it gave me
the clearest insight I had yet had into the mind of the
average Irish peasant.

"Ye see, ma'am," said Paddy at last, or the gillie, I
forget which, but they both echoed each other; "it just
comes to this. Here's my bit of land"—drawing the outline of it on the sandy bank with his stick. "My father,
an' his father before him, paid a pound a year rent for
it—built the cottage, cut the turf, and made the bog into
good ground—which takes a while to do. Then the landlord raises my rent to two pounds—and three pounds.
An' I can't pay; for potatoes and oats—oats and potatoes—without any change of crops, makes the land poor.
And times is bad, and stock low. A cow my father got
eight pound for, I couldn't sell this year for four pound.
Everything's fallen—except the rent. If the landlord
would wait—now some landlords have waited, and got
their rents, in many parts of Donegal—but some won't
wait, and then—what's to be done?"

Alas! wiser folk than either they or I would find it difficult to answer that question.

"But you don't hate your landlord — even though he may be a Protestant?" For the most part of the large land-owners in Ireland, and especially in this part of Ireland, are Protestant — and I knew the two men were Catholics, as I had seen Paddy take off his hat at the sound of the Angelus. "You would not harm him? You wouldn't wish ill to me either — even though I am a Protestant?"

"Not a bit of it, ma'am," returned Paddy, with a laugh. And then the gillie — a much younger and shrewder man, began, and preached, in his simple fashion, one of the best sermons on charity that I had heard for years, clinching his doctrine by texts out of the Bible — which, Catholic as he was, he evidently had at his fingers' ends — and winding up by an exordium which, in its homely earnestness, would have done credit to any pulpit.

"Then you don't want to fight England?" I said.

"No, we'll gain nothing by fighting. There's a gentleman named Parnell, he says we'll soon get everything we want. He has got a lot of money, they say, but I don't know that he has got anything else. If times would mend the landlords would be paid their rents."

"An' Catholics and Protestants would live peaceably together," added Paddy, who had listened to his companion with much respect. "But we'd betther start now, ma'am, if ye're to see the Marble Church and the Poison Glen."

We did see both—though with difficulty, and only by

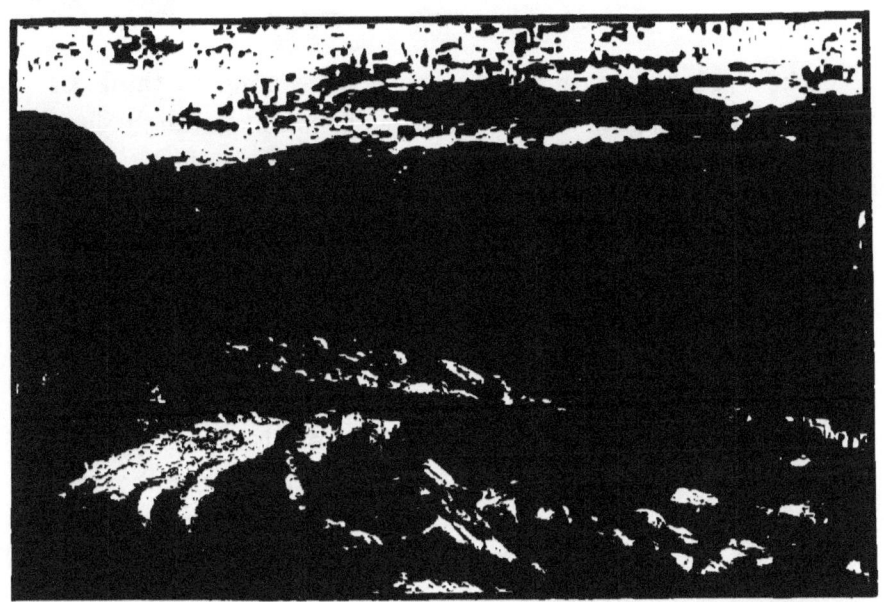

THE POISON GLEN.
(*From a Drawing by* F. NOEL PATON.)

the gillie carrying each one of us, Atlas-like, on his strong
back, ashore. At the head of the lough stood the pretty
little church, built by some indomitable Protestant, we
heard, for a regular congregation—of three persons! The
Catholics had proposed to buy it, but this was refused, and
the bishop was coming to consecrate it next week. I hope
the future pastor, whoever he is, will preach sermons as
pacific and Christian as that of the poor, uncultured gillie
whom I had heard this day.

Poison Glen—which our artist came and drew, surrounded by an army of midges, and a few human beings,

who eyed him with great suspicion, seeming to think he had something to do with the police—is exceedingly fine. However, it was such stiff walking that we did not penetrate far. Afterwards, there was nothing to do but to row home; which we did in a gorgeous sunset, that transfigured Erigal into a mountain of light. On its very top we saw two black figures emulating our adventurous climbers of two nights before—of whom, I should add, that, with one of the frequent coincidences of travel, as soon as they told us their names, we found we knew their family quite well, as they knew us. They went on to Carrick; and their vacant places were soon filled up at the. friendly hotel-table. But I think they will not soon forget Gweedore.

Nor shall we forget the long, quiet, lazy day when we did nothing, only, like the apostles, and good old Izaac Walton, "went a-fishing."

PART VI.

SEPTEMBER 4th.—Another Saturday already! Our days here were numbered.

I hardly know in what consists the charm of Gweedore. It is scarcely picturesque, in an artistic sense; has no gloomy glens or tumbling streams; and its one mountain —Erigal—stands up straight as a sugar-loaf or a beehive from the surrounding moor. But a charm it has, which we all of us felt, and sighed to think how soon we must leave this happy valley, full of sunshine and sweet air; which has, to hard workers, the same felicitous combination as the Happy Valley of "Rasselas"—that you can get at nobody, and nobody can get at you. At least, not without considerable difficulty.

Which makes its inhabitants, permanent or temporary, all the more sociable and kindly. Our landlord took as much interest in our proceedings as if we had belonged to him. And the owner of the salmon fishery, a gentleman quite unknown to us, who had before offered us his gillie, now benignly insisted on taking us in a boat on a day's picnic to one of the several islands which lie in the bay opposite Bunbeg.

So off we started under his charge—a party of five—minus our artist, who preferred duty, midges, and the Poison Glen—which he afterwards sincerely regretted; for this was one of the pleasantest days in all our tour. Merrily we drove to Bunbeg, stopping on the way to see the salmon-leap, which by the energy of our friend has been utilized for one of the few industries that Donegal can boast — salmon - fishing. Reaching the quay, we found waiting, with the same grave, taciturn, but kindly air, our guide of two days before — who looked equally surprised to see his unknown guests. We all greeted one another cordially.

"So you know my friend John Williams—manager of my fisheries, magistrates' clerk at Bunbeg, and one of the best fellows going? Well done, John. I see you've got us the *Jessie*—a capital boat she is. We'll have a splendid sail."

It was splendid. What a fascination—to good sailors—there must be in yachting; not your commonplace but convenient steam yacht, but a boat with sails; skimming over the water like a bird, first dipping on one side and then on the other, and again scudding, arrow-like, straight before the wind. The motion was so steady as well as delightful that even we land-lubbers thoroughly enjoyed it; and wished, granted the same conditions, that we could have sailed on and on—say to the North Pole!

But we didn't. After a few tacks we glided safely into

a narrow channel between the islands of Gola and Umphin; on the latter of which we landed.

One can easily understand the superstitious feeling which has left, on our northern coasts especially, so many " holy " islands, chosen as hermitages, monasteries, or burial-places. This little rocky dot in the midst of the wild sea, so small that in ten minutes you could walk over it from end to end—uninhabited, except by sea-birds, and without a trace of any human visitant—was a most attractive place. Seaward the rocks seemed to rise to a considerable height, but towards the land they sloped down in little dells covered with the richest grass, and which in spring must be full of flowers. Westward, there was an ascent across the top of a natural archway or bridge, from which you looked down — a dizzy depth — at the waves which came tumbling in and recoiling; beating their way as they had beaten it for uncounted centuries through the hard rock. A place which no one who loved, or had ever loved, a scramble could resist. It was like the days of one's youth, to stand on this slender bridge and watch the boiling waters below, and then look over to the opposite island of Gola, and to the glittering sea beyond. And rather hard it was to descend by the green slope aforesaid, in the midst of which bubbled out a tiny spring — where on earth can this fresh water on small rock-islands come from?—and condescend to a comfortable, ordinary lunch, in front of that lovely picture framed by the hand of Nature.

John Williams, who with two other men had been left to beach the boat, soon joined us, and gave us all the

information he could about the island, which was little
enough, for Umphin, like Skull Island, seems to be without a history.   But he was very strong on the subject of
the Spanish ship, again pointing out the place where he
was certain she lay, since at low water she was so near the
surface that the fishermen declared they could have stood
upon her hull! and the rusty anchor had been seen, not
only by himself, but by an old woman still living at Bunbeg.

Nothing could shake his testimony on this point, but
we could get no more out of him as to Skull Island.   He
told us " a young gentleman" had been there sketching it,
and had found " the person," as he persisted in calling our
skeleton.   He did not tell us what the young gentleman
(our artist) had told us already—that John Williams had
stood gravely by and let it be found, without hinting that
it had been dug up and carefully reburied only the day before!   Probably other tourists may go through the same
performance — unless some of them may pause lest the
ghost that was once a living man should follow them with
Shakespeare's malediction,

> "Curst be he that moves my bones."

John Williams's individuality interested me much.   He
was, he had told me, of Welsh parentage, born on Rathlin
Island.   He had lived all his life in these parts, where, being a Protestant and a magistrates' clerk, he was a sort of
representative of the " law and order" side.   Consequently
he had his enemies—especially among poachers.   But the

courage and daring of the man, his employer told me, were wonderful. He was literally afraid of nothing. In his duty as manager of the salmon-fishing he often had to run great risks. Once, seeing some poachers throwing a net across the stream, he jumped right into it and allowed himself to be dragged ashore—when he found himself face to face with six men. But they were unarmed, and he had his revolver. He pointed it at them and they ran away. John did not follow them, having no wish to harm them, but contented himself with marching off with the net on his shoulder—which, being a costly thing, he knew would effectually prevent more poaching for many a day.

Though well on in life, his physical strength and activity are unabated. Missing him for a minute or two from the conversation, I suddenly saw him half-way up the rock, towards the archway, climbing with a rapidity and seeming recklessness that made me shiver.

"Oh, he has gone after that plant you noticed. Don't trouble yourself about him, he is as sure-footed as a mountain goat—all our men are. They scale the rocks as boys after sea-birds' eggs. Bravo, John!" as he descended with the plant in his hand—one I had never seen before. "This lady thought you were killing yourself. That was a steep climb though. You're a young man still, I see."

John smiled, and accepted my thanks with great indifference. But I determined never again to notice curious plants that grow on precipices.

After this — safely guided — we did a deal of climbing ourselves. Ascending to the highest point in the little

island, and finding there a ledge of rock, like a sofa, only a
trifle harder, we all sat down to contemplate the sea-view,
only ending with the horizon. There is always something
solemn in the bright blankness of a sea without ships. We
were involuntarily

" Silent as on a peak in Darien,"

until John Williams, who had seated himself a little way
off, with his usual air of respectful independence, pointed
out two or three little black dots tossing about on the
water.

" Look, sir, there are the curraghs! The Sligo steamer
will be round shortly."

And then we heard about these curraghs—boats of
canvas stretched over wicker, something like the leather-
covered coracles of the ancient Britons—which are used
for fishing, and for carrying fish to and from the steamboats that sail periodically, at a safe distance, round this
dangerous coast. Soon we perceived the slender line of
smoke which indicated that the Sligo steamer was coming
round the point—of Owey Island, I think they said—or
the end of the Isles of Arran, which have been so much
written about in the newspapers, and where I should
much have liked to go, but it would have been an expedition perfectly impracticable.

What a strange, wild scene it was! We, sitting aloft
on this solitary place, and the cluster of boats rocking
below, waiting for the little steamer that was their one
link of commerce and civilization. As if in contrast to

it all, the gentlemen proposed that we should fancy ourselves on the grand stand at the Derby, and have a sweep-
stake—the prize being a packet of chocolate—to be won
by whoever guessed correctly the time when the steamer
would reach a certain point nearest to us. Great laughter and joking there was, when the Barbarous Scot, who
might be "Old Time" himself in his remorseless accuracy
and punctuality, sat, watch in hand, proclaiming not only
minutes, but seconds, as the little vessel steamed on.

"She has stopped! No! Yes, she has—for the boats
are all gathering round her. Now—who has won?"

I think it was the Wild Irish Girl, who was very proud
of her luck. We laughed a good deal, and ate the chocolate, and examined the steamer with a spyglass; wondering much if the crew were examining us, and what
they thought of the sight—seven human beings sitting,
like a row of sea-gulls, on the topmost rock of this uninhabited island!

Very childish it all was, and yet very pleasant. Years
hence, when the young folks are grown old, and the old
folks—well! never mind that! it may be pleasant still to
remember that lonely peak of Umphin Island and the
little Sligo steamer creeping silently across the empty sea.

We sailed back, or rather rowed; for the wind had gone
down and we might otherwise have been hours in getting
home—sailed through a very fine sunset glow, against
which the ridges of rocks, fringed with a line of solemn-
looking sea-birds, were sharply defined. Also another
island, where were the remains of a gallows upon which

an Irish king is said to have been hanged; nobody seems to have died comfortably in his bed in those wild days. Then we skirted the outside edge of Skull Island, where a small boy sat on a ledge fishing, at the imminent risk of his life.

"But they will do it," said John, calmly—he had boys of his own. "Very likely he can swim like a fish—they all can."

"Yes—they are a hardy lot, and a fine lot, about here," said our host, who was an Englishman, but had grown familiar with the place and the people, among whom he spent so many months—and so much money—yearly. He seemed popular too. There cannot be a greater mistake than to suppose the native Irish hate the English. Theoretically — and in the aggregate — perhaps they do, when hatred is forced upon them; but individually, and when the individual behaves himself as "a man and a brother," he will almost always find himself received as such. Here, as elsewhere, it must be a tender hand as well as a strong and a firm one which has any power to guide a race turbulent and impulsive by nature, as untrained as wild horses, and yet a race equally noble, and equally capable of being made valuable, instead of dangerous, to the community at large.

Some time after, I received a letter from our kindly host of this day, in which he says: "I have lately found in the island of Owey a much more remarkable place than the natural archway you saw. It is a small, nearly land-locked bay, with one entrance through an arch of rock,

then an open channel, then a grand obelisk, a strange
natural imitation of Cleopatra's Needle. As nearly as our
rough calculating instruments could say, its height above
low water is eighty-six feet. I intend to photograph it,
and will send you a copy."

Evidently there is still a great deal to be discovered, by
enterprising minds and active bodies—in and near Gweedore.

Sunday, September 5.—Was a day of perfect beauty
and perfect rest. We drove to church for many miles
across the moorland, through a village or little town, as
it would be considered here, meeting group after group
going to chapel in their Sunday best—the frieze petticoat,
the bright-colored shawl, and generally another little ker-
chief tied over the head. The men too were decently
clad, and the demeanor of all was quiet and sedate—as
of people who respect themselves, and reverence their
Maker and his day. Such a number of them too—considering the sparse population. It seemed as if every
man, woman, and child had felt it a duty to go to mass,
clean and tidy, this Sunday morning; proving how enormous is the influence of the Catholic clergy, for good as
well as for evil. Alas, that so many of them should mis-
use it!

After a day spent among friends—a day which, looking back upon it, seemed all sunshine and sweetness,
freshness and flowers, for we were in the garden most of
the time, we saw, in returning, the same family groups,

13

sitting by the roadside on the moor, or chatting outside
their cabin doors. They just glanced up as we drove past
—nothing more. There was nothing of the wild pursuit
of tourists by child-beggars—and grown-up beggars too—
and nothing of the fierce scowl at all supposed well-to-do
people, which I had been told we should find in this land
ripe for revolution. And though they were as poor as
poor could be—a poverty which our English poor could
hardly realize—they all looked *respectable;* a word which
implies more than at first appears, since a man who is
worthy of respect must first respect himself. They would
have been a problem to many English who pass rash and
harsh judgments upon Ireland.

And so we watched the sun set on a scene that while
I write rises vividly before me, the endless miles of moor
and bog—we had grown to think bog-land beautiful—the
long chain of distant mountains, dyed all colors in the
evening light. It was our last evening at Gweedore.

Monday, September 6.—And a very black Monday too.
At breakfast-time the rain fell in such torrents that we
thought we should have to upset all our plans and stay.
We looked outwards on the soaked garden and inwards
to the streaming courtyard, then called into council Paddy
the fisherman, who gave the truly oracular opinion, "Maybe, sir, it'll rain all day, an' maybe it won't." Our kindly
landlord sympathized, but he too was perplexed, since if
we did not go this day he could not send us the next,
when every horse and car was requisitioned for the con-

secration of the Marble Church—the bishop being expected
here to-night. At last some of us saw, or thought they
saw, a break in the clouds, a lull in the rain, and urged
departure. So we departed.

I thought then—I think still—that it was a pity. Travellers should always leave a margin for weather. It would
have been wiser to wait for a good day, and then do the
whole journey between eight in the morning and eight
at night, which, with one relay of horses and a rest half-
way, is easily possible. From Gweedore to Carrick is
scarcely less than fifty miles, but it is a fifty miles of
such remarkable scenery as can be met with nowhere else
on the British Islands. Its utter desolation—far greater
than even between Letterkenny and Gweedore—strikes
one as something incredible, considering that it is actually only twenty-four hours' distance from London, the
heart of the civilized world.

With a wrench we tore ourselves from peaceful Gweedore, followed by a heap of good wishes for fair weather,
which fate scattered into empty air! We had crossed
Crolly Bridge, and were turning to look our last upon
Gweedore river, when the oldest and most anxious-minded
of us meekly suggested, "that it was beginning to rain
again." Of course the idea was scouted indignantly—at
first. Then, those who had waterproofs began to put
them on, and those who had hats likely to spoil secluded
them, and sported woollen caps instead. Umbrellas were
dispensed with for a while—they shut out the view, and,
though pleasant to yourself, are apt to drip unpleasantly

on your neighbor. In fact, I would suggest to travellers in Donegal that a good cloth waterproof—not one of those horrible shiny things, in every fold of which lurks a pool of water—a hood, and a long Scotch plaid over the knees, are better than any umbrella.

We saw our fate before us, and spent the first half-hour in disbelieving it, the second in fighting against it. Then we accepted it, with a noble cheerfulness which I must say never flagged during the whole thirty-five miles. Fortunately, we had a wagonet, not a car, so that our feet were warm, and being face to face we could laugh together at our misfortunes. As we did laugh, mile after mile, catching sunshine from the mutual good-humored acceptance of tribulation, which is the very heart of pleasant companionship in travelling.

But it could not be called a good journey or a lively road. First came a slight ascent crowned by a "village" —a few wretched cottages, at whose damp doors stood one or two women "so withered and so wild in their attire" that they reminded us of Macbeth's witches. Then a dreary inlet, or rather several inlets of sea, with sandy vegetation—Annagary Strand. Across it moved a dark spot, which we soon saw was a man on horseback, taking a short cut, half riding, half swimming his horse, to the opposite point. He was the only human interest we had for miles, and we watched him with much curiosity, thinking of Edgar Ravenswood in the last pages of the "Bride of Lammermoor." But ten times wilder than any scenery of Scott's is this of Ireland.

IN THE ROSSES.

(From a Drawing by F. NOEL PATON.)

The Rosses, into which we had now entered, is a district which for desolation has no parallel in Europe. Bounded by the sea on one hand, the Derry-Veagh Mountains and lesser hills on the other, its extent is equal to an English county—Rutland for instance. A single road crosses it, to a single village—Dungloe; but beyond this, no maps indicate it, no guide-books describe it. I wish I could! I wish instead of driving through in pelting rain, and seeing it by glimpses from under umbrellas, I could have walked it on my own two feet—young feet, alas! they needed to be—the fourteen miles to Dungloe, and the twenty-two more to Glenties! What a treat for an energetic pedestrian! for the road is very good, and on either side of it opens out a world of wonder and beauty: bog, moor, boulder, tiny mountain tarns, where heaps of trout are said to lurk, ignorant of rod or fly, and everywhere a solitude absolutely unbroken, an interminable wavy ocean of land, as empty and pathless as the sea.

He was a bold man who first planted in this wilderness the tiny town of Dungloe. For a town it is, and must have been for a good many years. The hotel we stopped at had large, old-fashioned, well-built sitting-rooms, and a long gallery of bedrooms, not uncomfortable, apparently. We got a good meal—of excellent fresh eggs, milk, bread-and-butter—also a piano, which was made to discourse excellent music while we rested; so far as we could rest, with the longest half of our journey yet to come. And then, under the joyful hope that it would be fair—for it really had ceased to rain—we again went out into the wilderness.

What a glorious wilderness it was! What a sky arched over it! Gray still, but brightened with patches of amber and rose, coloring the distant mountains, and reflected in every tiny lake. Our artist longed to stop and paint, but we might as well have left him like Robinson Crusoe on the desert island. And besides, grand as it was to look at, the scenery was too diffused and monotonous for the pencil. Or, indeed, for the pen. No description is possible. I can only say, Go and see.

We sat and gazed, silently almost, for I know not how many miles. In truth, one ceases to count miles here. They seem a variable quantity. One can half believe the story told to our artist, that the milestones are carried along in a cart, and wherever one of them happens to drop out, there it is set up. I can remember no special point in the landscape, no more than I could in the Atlantic Ocean—had I ever crossed it, which I never shall do now—until the carriage stopped at the top of a sharp descent; so sharp that we all voluntarily turned out, and saw below us a pretty little village and a picturesque river, the Gweebarra, rushing over rocks and boulders into Gweebarra Bay.

Here, at last, would be a lovely place to halt at; but halt we dared not, for the light was fading fast. Skirting the village, though not entering it, the road wound up again into another stretch of monotonous moor, except that even the heather gradually ceased, giving place to continuous masses of great boulders and smaller stones, thrown together in the most fantastic way. Never, except on the top of the Alps, have I seen such a total absence of any green thing. "Desolation of desolation" was written upon all around. And then somebody said, "Look at the west!"

Alas! the colors had all faded out, and a black after-sunset cloud—the sort of cloud one knows only too well in mountainous countries—was rising, minute by minute, covering the luminous sky. Very grand it was, with its trailing skirts gradually blotting out the horizon and coming nearer and nearer till it was down upon us.

I have been in a storm on the top of St. Gothard,

soaked to the skin. I have faced in Highland glens tempests so wild that one had fairly to sit down on the ground, draw one's plaid over one's head and wait till it was over. But I never remember such rain as this rain—not a downpour, but a deluge; not a wind, but a hurricane. It came sweeping along with a kind of fiendish howl, as if to say, "I have you now!" And truly it had. All idea of scenery went out of our minds; we became absorbed in the one thought of protecting ourselves and others. Sometimes, when little streams of water came trickling down our own backs, or our neighbors' noses, and there was a mild suggestion that umbrellas might be slanted so as to deposit their tiny cataracts outside instead of in the carriage, we broke into a hearty laugh at our misfortunes. But no one suggested that we had brought them on ourselves, and that by the exercise of a little patience and common-sense we might now have been peacefully sitting in our cosey parlor at Gweedore.

"Just think of this time yesterday, when we were walking in that sunshiny garden, gathering 'the last rose of summer,' which was far from 'blooming alone'—and eating peaches from the wall!"

Incredible—yet true. And I wish to state the fact as a warning to travellers. The present day, the present hour, is all you can count upon as to weather, and perhaps a few other things, in Ireland.

At last our driver, who had sat like a stone, the rain running down him and dripping off him, turned round.

"It's only two miles now to Glenties."

Never was news hailed with more delight. And though it took fully an hour to drive those long two miles, and when we got there we found neither fire nor food attainable for nearly an hour more, still, we had a roof over our heads and were thankful.

Two of us had been at Glenties before; this was our second visit. As for the third—well!

We spent fourteen hours in that memorable town—or village, or whatever you like to call it. But they are over. Let us not chronicle them. The good folks did their best —and so did we.

September 7th.—Ardara (the accent is on the last syllable), where we found ourselves at ten next morning—of course, an exceedingly and aggravatingly fine morning— is a very pretty place. At what exact point the district called the Rosses is supposed to end I know not; but after Glenties its peculiarities cease. It becomes fertile and green. Its desolation changes into cultivation, not of a very high type—first-class farming is unknown in Ireland, where if Nature does little, man does less. A patch of oats, a field of potatoes, a turf ridge for fence, and a fallen tree or an old ladder balanced on two heaps of stones to serve for a gate, this is what one continually finds. Irish ingenuity uses anything for any purpose, just as it comes to hand; and Irish laziness generally leaves it there. To expect the luxuriant pastures, hay-meadows, harvest-fields, and, above all, the neatly-kept hedgerows of England, or the highly-cultivated straths of Scotland, would be idle. Yet there are little oases here and there, and Ardara seemed to be one of them.

Glenties, the haunt of a few fishers and "commercial gentlemen," anciently called "bagmen," who are extremely welcome and valuable visitors in this far-away region, is not at all suited for tourists. Nothing can make it anything but—Glenties. But Ardara—which is very picturesque in itself, and close on the borders of a most picturesque country—would, if it had a first-rate hotel, be such a centre of travelling that it might command its own custom.

How many shops Ardara boasts I will not undertake to say. But I can answer for one good baker, of whom we purchased the lunch we had not dared to risk in Glenties; a capital loaf, divided into slices—which the said baker proposed to cut with a *hammy* knife—a pot of marmalade, and a spoon to eat it with, which gleamed like silver, price one penny. Our driver assured us we should find "plenty of wather" in the mountain streams, and we had several travelling-cups. So thus luxuriously provided against all emergencies, we started afresh, in the best of spirits and the brightest of sunshine.

Glen Gesh, which is not far from Ardara, is one of the sweetest glens I ever saw. Sweeter, perhaps, from the contrast its peaceful beauty was to the desolation we had passed through the day before. We ascended for a mile and a half in gradual windings, between two smooth slopes of fertile land. The bottom, vividly green, was sprinkled here with busy groups, making and carrying what seemed excellent hay. Hay in September sounds strange; but we

found it often still left in the fields. Every turn in the
road made a picture, framed between these two verdant
sides, of the distant Rosses and the mountains beyond—so
different from yesterday! If we had only waited for the
sunshine of to-day! But perhaps, after all, it was best.
We should otherwise never have realized the intense dreariness, the awful solitude of those not far-distant places
which to some of our fellow-creatures are "home"—the
only home they know, and to which they cling with a
tenacity' that to outsiders is utterly incomprehensible.

On the top of Glen Gesh we sat down to eat and drink,
blessing the little mountain stream and the baker of Ardara,
and looking back on a view which I can see still with shut
eyes, and remember as one of the lovely visions that we
carry away with us—forever. Afterwards the country
grew less interesting, and more civilized. There came a
village and a schoolhouse. We had seen, in the very heart
of the Rosses, a tumble-down cabin, over the door of which
was painted in straggling letters, "National School." But
this one was a good-sized cottage, and out of it poured at
least a dozen healthy-looking children—barefooted, bare-
headed, but with clean faces and sturdy brown limbs.
Nothing strikes one more in Donegal—or, indeed, throughout Ireland—than the exceeding wholesomeness of the
children. Ragged they may be, thin and half-starved, but
they are seldom either crippled or diseased. They can run
like hares, and spring like wild cats; they look up at you
fearlessly with their big, bright, Irish eyes, and grin at you
with their dazzling white teeth, till you laugh in spite of

yourself, and they laugh back again, as if, in spite of all this misery, life were a capital joke.

Half a dozen of these—the young generation of Ireland, of which hundreds are drafted off weekly to America and the Colonies—followed us for a mile or more, tempted by the remnants of our lunch, especially the marmalade-pot, and a newspaper, thrown out of the carriage for mischief, and eagerly seized by one urchin, as if he had never seen such a thing in his life before. Then we left them behind and hastened on towards Carrick. For the day was already darkening, and the mountains, which again began to rise round us, were misty with approaching rain.

Down it came, blotting out hills, glens, sea—we knew we must be near the sea. How many lovely views we missed I cannot tell. We had to take all on faith. And when we arrived like drowned rats at Carrick—of which we had heard such glowing accounts that we had made it the climax, and end, of our expedition—we felt that, in spite of all the allurements of scenery, a warm fire, a good dinner, a cosey parlor, and a capital piano are no small items in the aggregate of human felicity.

Wednesday, September 8th.—Here I again hesitate whether or not to cross the sacred line which ought always to divide public from private life. But the Musgraves of Carrick are so widely known, and have been so much talked about and written about, that I shall hardly do harm in mentioning them, and our personal experience of them; they being hitherto unknown to us.

Rising this morning to a day so doubtful that we held an after-breakfast council as to what we should do—if we could do anything—there was announced a visitor; an elderly gentleman, hale and hearty, the raindrops glistening on his gray frieze shooting-coat and pleasant rosy face —who gave us "welcome to Carrick." He was Mr. John Musgrave, head of a well-known Belfast firm, and eldest of a large family of brothers and sisters, all unmarried, who had been reported to us as using their large income in doing "a power o' good."

A good many years ago, being accidentally at Carrick, he and his brother took a great fancy to the district; bought land, built a shooting-lodge, then bought and enlarged the little inn, adding acre to acre as opportunity offered, until now they own the whole country-side, and are among the large land-owners whom the preachers of the doctrine of "three acres and a cow" so much decry. But what have they done with their land? They have built cottages upon it; made roads through it, which cost thousands of pounds, and then assigned them over to public use; have helped to get the harbor repaired, and the fisheries restarted; have instituted various inland industries, besides employing a host of people, and giving them steady wages through hard times. In short, they have done all that clever business men, with their hearts in the country, could do, to benefit it.

Of course, they have had their calumniators—requiring to fight inch by inch against the ignorance which resists any improvement, and the prejudice which is always ready to discover an ill motive rather than a good one. They have had to cast their bread upon the waters, with the certainty of *not* finding it, even after many days. But they have gone on from year to year, succeeding or failing, as might happen, yet always undismayed. "The Musgraves" are known and respected all over Donegal.

Much of this we had already heard; during the next few days we saw it with our own eyes.

Well, and what shall I show you? If you don't mind a wetting—we never do at Carrick—the salmon-leap will be splendid in this rain. And then you can drive down to the harbor and the coastguard station. We must wait a fine day for Slieve League, whether you go there by land or sea."

Now Slieve League was one of the places I had visited fifteen years before, and one of the chief aims of my present visit was to see it again. It is a grand mountain —we saw from our parlor window its huge black shoulder, down which the rain came sweeping in misty clouds, then clearing off for an hour or so, and then beginning again. One of its sides is, to seaward, a sheer precipice of perpendicular rock. You may walk to the edge, or creep on all-fours if your head fails you, and look straight down two thousand feet to the boiling waters below. I did it then, and have never forgotten the sight. I meant to do it again, and also to take a boat—only possible in very calm weather—and look at the cliffs upwards from below.

Mr. Musgrave at this suggestion shook his head, but

cheerily — he seemed a man who would take everything cheerily. "No Slieve League to - day, I think; but to-morrow, or the next day, to give this storm time to abate —you might try a boat; I'll manage it for you. Mean-time, you can do the harbor. And I should like to take you to a cottage where they are finishing a web of frieze —like this coat of mine—the best thing possible for our climate, for it never lets the wet in, and never wears out."

Of course we went. There has been much talk lately about Irish cottage industries, so solidly useful as well as dainty and beautiful. If English people could but see the cottages out of which they come, and the appliances for their manufacture! A cotton or cloth factory, with its perfect machinery and its clever "hands," educated therein from childhood, is one thing; an Irish cottage loom is quite another. When I looked at the small cabin and its five busy workers — two men and three women, the latter sitting silent over most delicate embroidery—I wondered at the humble means which resulted in such a good end. Whether the Irish peasant has the accuracy, persistency, and biddableness — to coin a word — requisite for the making of a good factory worker, is an open ques-tion; but decidedly he has a head that can work for it-self, and think for itself, with very satisfactory results. Here again — as I watched these poor folk, laboring on with such small appliances, there was borne in upon me a sense of the great capacity of the Irish race, if only it could be put to some practical use.

The river, varying enormously in size, according to
weather, runs down from Carrick village to the sea, between a perfect forest of Osmunda ferns, and over a
pretty salmon - leap. Thither we went — in waterproofs
and under umbrellas — Mr. Musgrave in his gray frieze
being nobly independent of either. And then, in a pause
of rain, we drove down to the harbor and pier he had
told us of; which, during hard times, had been built by
government to provide work for starving men, and to as-
sist the fisheries of Teelin Bay. Close beside it, on a little rocky hill, kept as neat as a garden, was the coastguard station and its tiny "lookout." Thence one of the
men descended, to help us up the steep path.

"Yes," he said, "that's the harbor, and the little pier
with the boats — very good boats too, if they were ever
washed and looked after. The fishermen will stand, day
after day, watching us wash ours, but they never do it
themselves. They just hang about, as you see them now
— talk, talk, talk. If you're wanting any of their boats,
ladies, you'd better think twice"—with a significant sniff
—"you mightn't like it."

The man was English, evidently; and his lookout —
built of the solidest material, and with the smallest of
windows, so as to resist storms, compared to which the
one we now sheltered from must have been mere child's
play — was as clean and tidy and in as good repair as
English hands, and sailors' hands, could make it. We all
"snuggled" therein, for our friend seemed pleased to welcome strangers, and still more so to discover that his

SALMON-LEAP AT CARRICK.
(*From a Drawing by* F. Noel Paton.)

native place was only a few miles from that of the Brown Bird and the Violet; so that he knew their name and all about their family. He had his little boy beside him— clean and wholesome-looking in the neatest of clothes, indicating a careful mother.

"Yes, my wife's English too. She belongs to South- ampton. She found it a great change coming here, where she's not got a soul to speak to, and can't go shop- ping" (shopping indeed! at Slieve League!). "But she's reconciled to it now. It's a healthy place, and the people here are not bad folks—if they'd only be a little more tidy."

14

We noticed the perfection of tidiness and cleanliness in his lookout.

"Ay, ay, we're obliged to keep things shipshape, for the inspector may be down upon us any day. He goes his rounds, giving no notice beforehand, and hears any complaints we have to make. We are not kept many years in one place—if it's a place like this we couldn't stand it. And we mostly have our wives and children with us"—patting kindly the flaxen head that hid behind him. "He's shy, ladies—he sees almost nobody here—but he'll mend by and by."

As no doubt he will—for he was a fine little fellow. May he grow up into one of those picked men who form our coastguard—whose dull daily life is almost as heroic as the deeds which now and then color it with a glow of self-forgetful courage that revives one's faith in human nature—the human nature which has the divine element at its core after all.

On this and the following day we heard a good deal about the fisheries. Of course, contradictory accounts. One was, that no fishing worth speaking of was to be got; the finny family, always a capricious race, having deserted their old haunts, or been driven away by the trawlers, so that it is necessary to go after them fifteen or twenty miles out to sea; which, for want of proper boats, the fishermen dare not do. The opposite side insists that there are plenty of fish to be caught, but no men skilful enough, or industrious enough, to catch them; that though government has built harbors and piers, and even given boats and nets, the boats lie idle, the nets hang rotting beside the cottage doors.

Probably the real truth lies between these two opposite versions of it. That the fish have migrated farther from the coast, and the fishing requires greater skill, and better appliances than are forthcoming, is tolerably sure. A recent government commission gives unquestionable statistics on the subject. Reporting of Killybegs — only a few miles distant from Teelin—it says :

"Mackerel appeared in great quantities and remained during July, August, and September, but a few only were caught, owing to the scarcity of nets. Lobsters and crabs were in great abundance. Soles were never caught at all till the trawlers came. It is impossible to calculate the enormous loss of fish for want of the proper means of capture."

Yet the report goes on to record : "Loans to fishermen (of six counties) during the past ten years ending December 31, 1884, £28,000. Repaid, £20,062. Out of two hundred and sixty - four applications for grants to construct or improve boat-steps, piers, harbors, fifty-four were inquired into and fifty - five recommended, the cost being roughly estimated at £193,000."

After this who shall say that England refuses to help Ireland, or that Ireland never pays her debts? If the politicians of both countries would cease talking and act ; if the people would give up wrangling and work ; if the upper classes would show an example to the lower, instead of censuring them for not possessing virtues which for centuries their betters have too seldom exemplified, thrift, order, carefulness, reticence of language, uprightness of life, and, above all, Christian charity—then indeed there might be some hope for Ireland.

September 9th.—We woke up to the wildest storm. Slieve League in the distance looked black as Acheron. Down the road leading to Carrick village the rain swept in a deluge. Opposite, two or three men were trying to save the poor remainder of a hay-stack, half of which, though it was tied down with ropes, had been already blown away. At 8 A.M. everything outside seemed hopeless, but at twelve there was a break in the clouds, a lull in the wind and rain, and presently Mr. Musgrave appeared.

"Get your lunch as quickly as possible. I have brought my car and ordered another. I want to take you to Muckross. It will be fair. Oh, yes! it is sure to be fair."

His sanguine energy was too much for us. We meekly obeyed, and were soon under way; whither we knew not, but everywhere was interesting.

Muckross is a rocky peninsula forming one of the horns of the little Bay of Killybegs, which is included in the grand half-circle of Donegal Bay. We drove to it along the high mountain-road above the salmon-river, which runs into the sea at Teelin. This road, planned and carried out by the Musgraves at their own expense, in a time of great distress, and then made over by them

THE LAIR OF THE WHIRLWIND.

to the government, is one of the finest imaginable. Every few yards of it gives a different view of mountain and sea. The country it winds through, though so grand, is not desolate like the Rosses. Every now and then we passed a small holding—cottage, potato-garden, and a field or two, sometimes with a cow on it—and in one instance we saw a woman industriously shaking out hay with her two hands, which is the Donegal fashion of "tedding."

And then, in the intervals of saying "How grand!" "How beautiful!" of which one sometimes wearies a little, I gathered much information, in which, as in most other instances, I carefully avoid identifying the facts with those from whom I heard them. But that I did hear them from reliable sources, and have recorded them accurately, I must ask my readers to believe.

"They are a fine race, these Donegal peasants?" I said, as when we stopped two big, strong men came forward to hold the horses, and each offered a brown, dirty, friendly hand, not only to those they knew, but to me, the stranger.

"Not a finer race under the sun; honest, sober, moral, intelligent. Most of them, besides their farm-work, do their own building, thatching, and weaving. Little money is current among them — they exchange butter and eggs for the few articles they want at the shops. Many of them never stir all their lives from the spot where they were born, but some go over to America as pedlers, make a little money, come back and sink it in land. The 'land-hunger' is an ineradicable passion in the Irish heart."

" And the ' love of the sod ' its strongest emotion ?"

" Yes, because our Irish farms are not like your English ones. Here, the tenant generally has built his own house, reclaimed his own land; consequently he feels as if he had a right to it, and clings to it in a way incomprehensible to your English peasant. When his children grow up he subdivides it among them, but as there is seldom any industry possible outside the farm, they cannot live upon it. The land will not support its population—they must emigrate or starve."

" And how about evictions?"

" A good resident landlord will avoid evictions if possible. He can generally distinguish between those who can't pay, and those who won't pay, and act accordingly."

Seeing how stalwart and healthy-looking were the men we met, in spite of all their rags, I asked about that great curse of a nation—drunkenness; remarking that except at Ballycastle Fair I had not seen a single drunken man in Antrim, Coleraine, or Donegal.

" No; as a rule they don't drink much—except at fairs, which occur far too often. The first day is for buying and selling, the second is for amusement—when the girls come from miles round for shopping and dancing. There's plenty of fun going, but it is decent fun. The worst sins of our people hereabouts are poaching and illicit whiskey-making. If on the mountains you meet a man with a gun, or see signs of a hidden ' still '—well! perhaps you had better—look another way !"

I might have owned to unlawful sympathies—inasmuch

as I never could quite understand why the fowls of the
air and the fish of the water should not be public property,
or why a man should not make his own whiskey as well as
his own soup, if he chooses—but these heterodox ideas were
suddenly quenched by our reaching Muckross. How, having
exhausted all available adjectives in painting many a previous picture of this splendid coast, shall I attempt another?

A long, narrow tongue of land, ending in seaweed-cov-
ered rocks—most difficult walking—and a ledge, where we
at last sat down—the wind made it impossible to stand—
with the black outline of Slieve League before us, and close
at our feet the enormous Atlantic rollers pouring in, dashing themselves into a deluge of spray, and scattering spin-
drift in large white flakes for many yards. Close by—
strange relic of past generations—was a small heap which
we were told was a Danish fort, but nobody seemed to
know much about it. The roar of the waves, the fierce
northwesterly wind, which was like battling against a
stone wall, the leaden-gray sky, the wild "white horses"
that kept leaping up even in the comparatively sheltered
Donegal Bay—one of the finest bays in Ireland, with its
single small island lying flat as a fish on the surface of the
water—all make up a scene which, if we never see it again,
we shall none of us ever forget.

We had scarcely time to take it in, before the angry
clouds above Slieve League warned us that we had better
think of departing. So, hurrying past Muckross village—
two or three cabins huddling under a cliff, where the peninsula joins the mainland—and refusing the universal hospi-

tality of "a dhrink of milk"—such delicious milk it is too!
—we remounted our cars.

A mile or two more, retracing the same coast road,
which at every turn took a new aspect of dreary sublimity
—and the storm was down upon us. The picturesque was
forgotten, and all our energies absorbed in the combined
effort of holding on and keeping dry.

Nobody seemed to mind it, least of all our good friends
in the gray frieze; who explained to us with unabated cheerfulness that this was "only the equinox," and after a week
or so of it would come the Donegal summer, the finest
time of all the year. "But," viewing the waves that rolled
in mountains high, against the entrance of Teelin Bay,
"you'll not be able to see Slieve League from a boat to-
morrow."

The Celt is not a coward; nor, if taught to work, is he
either a dunce or a sluggard, especially out of Ireland; but
in it, what with its soft, enervating, southern and tempest-
uous northern climate, he has a good deal to fight against.
These things ought to be considered in giving him the
comprehending sympathy without which there can be no
true justice. I gave it, in degree, to the poor fellows who
were hanging about the pier, in compulsory idleness. Oh!
that there could be put into them a little of the thirst for
work, and the love of it, which has carried the stolid Saxon
triumphantly into every corner of the world!

September 10.—And a tempest still. Well for us that
we were so snugly housed, with comforts that justified all

we had heard of Carrick Hotel. Manfully, and womanfully, we faced our woes. The shiny mackintoshes so objectionable for driving—since every fold involved a waterspout—were invaluable for walking. Hats being impossible, and umbrellas a delusion and a snare, the Barbarous Scot produced a welcome store of Tam-o'-Shanters, which he distributed all round; and very nice the merry young faces looked under them. Even I, in a costume emulating the Witch of Endor, at last followed the rest out into the storm.

Close by was the open door of the Catholic chapel; why are not our church doors always open? We entered, the Violet and I, and found it a handsome, simple building, still unfinished. Service had been carried on at a side altar, which was decorated with two large white figures, in much better taste than the tawdry shabbiness one often sees. Ladders and tools were lying about, and a young workman was busy at the rails of the high-altar, which were tasteful specimens of woodwork. He looked up with a civil "Good - morning," and we began talking. He was very intelligent, and his English, though sometimes a little foreign in construction, was exceedingly pure.

"Yes, it's beautiful wood, ma'am; wreckage — often a lot of it comes ashore here, mahogany, walnut, and pine; and is bought very cheap, as Father" —— (I forget his name) "bought this. He thinks it should be painted, but I'd like varnish better." And we here had an eager discussion, ending decidedly in favor of varnish. Pleased at our interest in him, he became confidential. "It'll be a fine

chapel when it's done, won't it, ma'am? I come and work
at it every day; but I'm not a Carrick man—I'm from
Ardara. Ye'll have seen Ardara?"

We gratified him by admiring the place, and he launched
out in praise of it; of the capital inn it had, with divergen-
cies to the landlord and his family history. The young
fellow's earnest, intelligent enthusiasm over his work, and
his simple confidence that we shared it, touched our hearts,
and though we never learned his name nor anything about
him, we carried away a good remembrance of the workman
of Ardara.

"National school," said the Violet, pointing to a large
cottage behind a potato garden, over the door of which this
was inscribed. "Let us try it. We shall be under a roof,
anyhow."

And without prejudice let me say that among the
many school-roofs I have been under, in England and Scotland, I never found a better shelter, mental and bodily, for
the young generation. It was a warm, well-ventilated,
wholesome room, filled, but not crowded, with children of
all sizes and ages, boys and girls together; apparently kept
in perfect order by the master, and one or two elder girls
as monitors.

They looked surprised at our sudden entrance, but the
master came forward with true Irish politeness, and when I
explained that we were strangers who took much interest
in education, he called up a class, and tested it in two out
of "the three R's"—reading and writing—most satisfactori-
ly. Then he asked us to take another class ourselves, and

I heard them read, verse and verse about, Southey's poem of "The Holly-tree;" the meaning of which, when questioned, these little barefooted, bright-eyed brats had taken in, I found, with surprising quickness. Then I sent them on imaginary map-journeys half over the world; they travelled intelligently, and showed a familiarity with the surface of the globe, and its productions, which was very creditable to their teacher.

He told me he had been here fifteen years, so that he must have come to Carrick as a mere boy, and these were his first scholar's children. They came, he said, from some distance round; though there is generally a National school within two or three miles, everywhere, all over Ireland. Many brought their little brothers and sisters, for warmth and safety, if not for schooling.

"They don't harm us," he said, looking over kindly to a group, you could not call it a class, of small, ragged, but perfectly clean roly-poly creatures, the eldest of whom could not be more than three years old. "They're good children, and their elders take a deal of care of them."

His chief trouble, he said, was that he could not keep his scholars long enough at school. Their parents, many of whom spoke only Irish, saw no good in English, or in any learning, and wanted them at home, the boys for farm-work, the girls for knitting. Still, they do contrive to learn something, and their bright, intelligent faces, big round arms and legs, contrasted vividly with the pale, skinny, wizened, gin-poisoned children that one sees in a London board school.

The Irish National schools arc, I learned afterwards, almost exclusively due to, and guided by, the Roman Catholic half of the population. These had demanded a purely secular teaching, while the Protestants insisted on a religious (and Protestant) education, consequently the scheme fell to pieces. The Catholics took it up and carried it through—though, by government rules posted up in every schoolroom, the teachers are bound not to interfere in any way with either politics or religion. Therefore, though, as I afterwards heard, the schoolmaster of Carrick is a rigid Catholic and a vehement Home-Ruler, I conclude he does not force his opinions upon his young flock any more than he did upon me. I hope he will cherish a kindly recollection of the two stranger ladies who went away as anonymously as they came.

Rain—rain—all day long. A faint pause in it took our artist out in search of work—and us of pleasure—along the road to Malin Head, which the Barbarous Scot, who protests that he enjoys dreariness, found quite to his mind. More to our minds was the bright turf-fire, and the social evening, when we made the very best of things, and went to bed with a glimmering of hope—for there were at least three stars visible over black Slieve League—to awake in despair.

For—at 6 A.M. on Saturday, September 11th—the rain was raining faster than ever. Our first news on descending was that our good landlord's hay-stacks had been carried clear away down the river, together with three sheep and two cows—I will not vouch for the numbers, which grew in every repetition.

"We shall never get to Slieve League—anyhow, *she* won't!" was the remark, with a reproachful glance at me, as if I were to blame for the weather in this place which I had brought them so far to see.

I did what I could; keeping up all day a cheerful fire and countenance; seeing to the periodical drying of water-proofs, which hung in a long row, like Blue Beard's wives; and suggesting the blessings—not universal—of a roof over our heads, a warm room, and a good dinner. And though it is difficult to keep one's temper under such circumstances, I wish to put it emphatically on record that we—the whole six of us—kept ours.

Sunday, September 12th.—And our last—for in two days our tour must end. Truly, in Irish weather as in French politics, nothing happens but the unexpected—for we rose to a day of perfect calm and heavenly sunshine!

While we stood listening to the chapel bell, watching the long stream of decently clad people going to mass—and considering whether, in the absence of other worship, we should not go in and say our prayers with them—a message came from the Musgraves saying that the car would come round and take us to the Protestant church at Glen Columbkille. So we went; along the same road by which we had driven towards Malin Head, but what a difference! The gray moor and black bog were bright with sunshine; the long, dark mass of Slieve League was tinted with all sorts of mountain lights and shadows; turn-ing off to the right, we came upon a very picturesque road,

and by and by we reached the glen, with a pretty church
nestling in its heart; semi-circular hills ending in abrupt
cliffs, sheltering it on three sides, and on the fourth a bright
outlook across the shimmering sea. We had forgotten all
the storms and blasts of the week—the world was beautiful
as ever.

Glen Columbkille is one of the endless memorials of
that remarkable man who has left the impress of his
character on both Ireland and Scotland. St. Columb's
Bed, a ruined tower on the headland opposite, and forty
"stations" marked with crosses within the glen, mark
where the saint had been. The original church, whose
foundations were discovered in digging a grave, was also
probably built by him, but, except the name, no tradition
remains of it. Nor of another curious "find"—a subter-
ranean passage sixty feet long, and consisting of three
chambers, which a workman's crowbar, struck into the
ground and disappearing, recently brought to light. Its
entrance, near the church-door, is now closed, but could
easily be opened again for the investigation of archæologists.

The simple service over, and the congregation of about
twenty people having melted away, we lingered in the
sweet, quiet churchyard—dating, no doubt, from St. Columba's time; for several very ancient crosses and fragments of tombstones were placed over the dead of later
generations. And among many nameless graves was one
beside which it was impossible to stand unmoved. It
was that of the young lieutenant, who commanded the

GLEN COLUMBKILLE.

(From a Drawing by F. NOEL PATON.)

Wasp, and was drowned with most of his crew, off Tory Island a few years ago — obeying orders, which, some people said, ought never to have been given. The simple headstone, recording only his name, age, and manner of death, looked white and fresh among the gray old graves —like a new grief among long-forgotten sorrows.

"Yes, it was a sad story," said the clergyman, show-

15

ing it to us. "His body drifted ashore not far from here. We knew it at once by the uniform. The men who found it had to carry it two hundred yards up the face of a steep cliff; then they fetched me. The coast-guard brought a coffin; we put him in it, just as he was, and I buried him."

"And his friends?" I said, for it is they one thinks of—the possible mother or sisters—or dearer still.

"They put up this stone, you see. And they were here not so very long ago, staying a few days in the glen. It is such a pretty, quiet spot."

"Yes," I said, and did not ask who "they" were, or indeed any more questions. It was all over now. Dead at twenty-two! But no man's life is too short when it ends while doing his duty.

I asked about the "stations."

"There is one," said the clergyman, pointing to a little hillock with a broken cross, before which two women knelt in absorbed prayer; then rose, and, taking no notice of us at all, threw their plaids over their heads and quietly went away. We passed them afterwards far down the road—walking gravely and silently. Both were young, and each had a rather sad face, as if there was something on her mind—one of those burdens that we all have to bear. If we can lay them down anyhow, anywhere—even at the foot of an old broken roadside cross—is it not well?

The way home was by Malin Head, past a lovely little bay, a coastguard station, and a few cottages, one of which

was pointed out to us as being, for half a summer, the
hermitage of Sir Frederick Leighton, P.R.A., where, in
his simple enjoyment of everything, he made no end of
friends. Not far off were some "giants' graves," as they
are called hereabouts—huge cromlechs, each with a double
or single circle of upright stones round it; slowly vanish-
ing, the farmers using them for cottage walls and fences.
However, as they now come under the shelter of Sir John
Lubbock's bill for the preservation of ancient buildings,
there will still be some archæological treasures left in
Donegal.

Our party—not being antiquaries—took more interest
in a salmon-ladder made in the river which ran through
the glen to the sea; and in a poor horse, seen struggling
in the bog.

ST. COLUMBA'S CROSS.
From a Drawing by F. Noel Paton.)

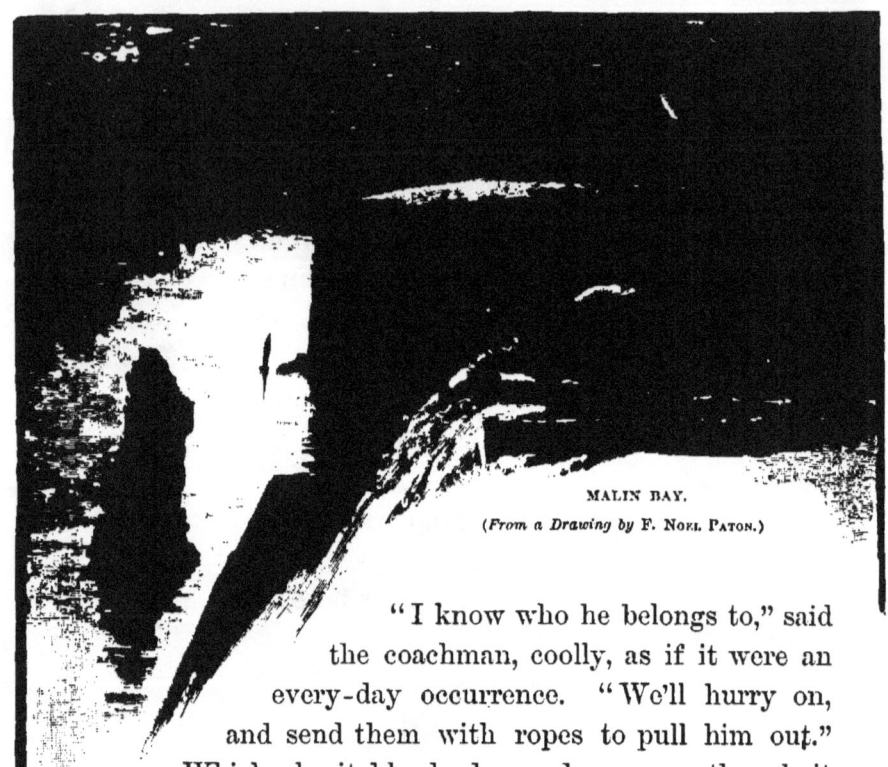

MALIN BAY.

(From a Drawing by F. Noel Paton.)

"I know who he belongs to," said
the coachman, coolly, as if it were an
every-day occurrence. "We'll hurry on,
and send them with ropes to pull him out."
Which charitable deed was done, even though it
was the Sabbath day.

And what a Sabbath! to the very last glimmer of
sunset light, which reddened even the far east! I went
out to catch it, and to inquire after the fate of the horse.

"He's all right, ma'am," said a cheery-looking woman,
standing at her door with two chubby boys; and she
explained that the owner was "up the mountain," but
that a man and girl from the next cottage had gone and
dragged the creature out. We had a little more talk, dur-

ing which the boys broke into a broad grin of recognition. "Ye'll please to excuse them, ma'am," the mother said, with a smile, "but ye spoke to them at the school."

Another family group was also enjoying its Sunday idleness, sitting on a turf-bank by the roadside. I stopped to speak to the smallest of them, an elf about four years old, who told me her name was "Mary," and kept fingering my clothes, repeating to herself, "Nice lady; nice gown! nice bonnet!" and (complacently patting it) "nice hand!" She had probably never seen gloves before. Her whole family—father, mother, and two big sisters—watched her proceedings with evident pride. They all looked so happy, so respectable, so far removed from public-house loungers and flaunting village girls, that I could believe entirely what had been told me in conversation a few hours before.

"If the priests teach many bad things" (the speaker was a woman, and a rigid Protestant), "they teach one good thing—purity. The very poorest peasants manage to keep up in their miserable cottages a wonderful modesty. They marry early, and live honest lives. Seldom does a husband desert his wife, and a lapse before marriage is among our girls a thing almost unheard-of."

Any one who knows what is the social condition of almost all English and Scottish villages will rate this fact at its just value in the present moral vitality and possible moral future of Ireland.

Yet she has her sins, original or invented. Which shall I call one sin? in the shape of two hares, carried

by our artist, who just then met me. He and a chance companion had been over Slieve League, where they saw two men with

ONE MAN'S PATH—SLIEVE LEAGUE.
(*From a Drawing by* F. Noel Paton.)

guns, who dropped the hares and ran; so they brought home the booty to the lord of the soil. Poaching, and on a Sunday too! What vice! But *that* vice, which, descending from the higher classes to the lower, ruins a nation in body and soul, eats out the heart of its strength, and makes it from head to heel one festering sore, that vice at least does not belong to Ireland.

Our artist, who had spent the whole day on Slieve League, spoke of it with enthusiasm. He had seen many a mountain, but none finer than this. Its sea flank, with the gigantic perpendicular cliffs; its dizzy One Man's Path, its long purple shoulder, with the little hollow where lay hidden the solitary lough, were all magnificent.

"You *must* go to-morrow; drive to Bunglas and walk the rest of the way. It's difficult, but not impossible. The cliffs would be .grandest from below, I think; but no boat could live there till the sea is quiet. Still, they are splendid from above. Such form, such coloring! You will so enjoy it!"

I knew I should. Our last day would be the climax of our tour. And in that delusion we all went to rest.

Monday, September 13th.—Our hopes died, unfulfilled. Six blanker faces than ours at breakfast could not readily be found. In-doors was a dull dampness which made everything feel clammy to the touch. Outside it was an "even downpour." Not a storm; there was no wind to blow the clouds away and make you feel that though raining cats and dogs one minute, it might possibly begin to clear the next. No; it was a quiet, determined, deliberate deluge. Hour after hour it went on; the sharpest, most sanguine eye could not detect one break in the leaden sky, one lull in the continuous flood.

We did not speak, or argue the question; we just sat down in silent despair. Some of us tried to work, as if by not thinking about it we should make the rain stop; and then we gave in entirely. After fifteen years of waiting and wishing to see Slieve League once more, after sitting for nearly a week at its very foot, after having brought my companions from the far end of England by my description of its beauties, we must go away and leave it unvisited. They were young, they might come again some day, but I? Old as I am, I could easily have added a drop or two to the deluge outside. Only, like poor Ophelia, we had "enough of water."

Well, who can fight against Fate? We read and talked eagerly, recklessly, upon several of the ethical subjects with which we were wont to beguile the time; every one expressing his or her opinion with a ferocious candor that left us all in exactly the same mind as we were at first; but conversation flagged and spirits likewise. At last, about 3 P. M., the Barbarous Scot could stand it no longer.

"Let us go to Slieve League, even if it's under umbrellas and in waterproofs."

The Brown Bird, who has pluck enough for anything, seconded the motion, and was followed, with a trifle less eagerness, by the Violet and the Wild Irish Girl. Our artist, notable for caution and courage alike, allowed that the expedition, though not pleasant, was possible. Of course, sacrificed himself upon the altar of chivalry with a cheerful countenance and offered to be the guide.

"You'll not see much, I fear, but you'll see something, and, anyhow, you can say you have been there."

So they started, the whole five, in costumes suited to the occasion, but which even now I laugh to think of, as I see them in my mind's eye setting off heroically from the hotel door. Only five; for if advancing years have their drawbacks, they at least teach us one thing, to "consume one's own smoke," as a friend of mine pathetically

puts it, and not to burden other people by attempting to
do what one knows one is not able to do. These two
maxims I beg to offer as the experience of a lifetime:
"Do all that you can, for as long as you can." And then,
"Accept the inevitable."

The party came back, just before nightfall, soaked to
the skin, and with boots that must be seen to be believed,
but in the best of spirits. Nobody had been drowned, or
lost in a bog, or blown off a cliff. And they had seen
all they could see and done all they meant to do; had
crawled to the cliff's edge and looked down the two thousand feet to the angry sea below; had traced the thin
line of "One Man's Path," though to tread it, slippery
with wet, would have been madness; and then had descended through sheets of driving rain, the mighty shoulder of the mountain.

"Very few tourists will see Slieve League as we saw
it," was the consolation in which they proudly hugged
themselves. And I fully agreed with them. If, as they
dilated on the wonderful grandeur of the spot, and how
even under those sad circumstances they would not have
missed seeing it on any account, I felt a lump in my
throat, knowing I must go away without seeing it, the
disappointment was pardonable.

September 14th.—What should we do with happiness
that comes too late? Most of us have known such a
thing, and its acute pain. Shall we sit down and cry over,
it? or grin and bear it? or make believe we don't really

care for it? or just pass it by in silence? I often think there is nothing sadder, or braver, than that couplet of Mrs. Barrett Browning's—true alike of small things and of great—

"Judge the length of the sword by the sheath's:
By the silence of life, more pathetic than death's."

This day, the day of our departure, was the end of the equinox, the beginning of the Donegal summer, and of weather glorious beyond telling. And yet—we had to leave; and we left.

Of course, I might have made what is called "a great fuss," have upset everybody's plans, inconvenienced about a score of people, and stayed. But our tour had lasted a whole month, and it was not wholly for pleasure, but for use. I had never meant to give exhaustive descriptions, or to make a Blue Book of facts, but to write what would interest English people and allure them to go and investigate Ireland for themselves. Therefore, since all the rest had seen Slieve League—some in sunshine, some in storm—I did not feel that it mattered much whether I myself saw it or not. So I resisted all kindly offers of a boat on the sea, or a pony on land, an expedition to Malin Head, and a picnic at beautiful Glen Columb-kille. Our artist was to stay behind and "do" all these things; which he did—as his work shows; but we others felt it right and best to depart.

One spare hour I spent in being piloted by a benevolent friend through Carrick Fair—dodging the horns of the little Donegal cows, and patting on their soft white

backs the pretty Donegal sheep, whose wool is the finest
in the world. And then the cars came to the door, and
our tour to an end. At least, so far as I shall write
about it, for the same evening we passed into private
life.

But our last drive together, from Carrick to Killybegs,
and from Killybegs on to Donegal and Lough Eske, was
one dream of loveliness from beginning to end. If, as we
heard, the Sligo steamer—the same that we watched from
Umphin Island on her weekly voyage to Derry — should
next year begin calling regularly at Teelin Bay for Carrick, it would open up to tourists a portion, unrivalled in
beauty and in interest, of that Unknown Country which
I have here tried to make known

And, I repeat, this book is merely a tour. It attempts
not to discuss the wrongs, the miseries, the sins of Ireland. But a state of things which has taken centuries
to fall into, may — I was going to write *must* — take centuries more to cure. I offer no opinions and suggest no
remedies. Nevertheless, while it is folly to cover with
court-plaster a running sore, or to ignore with ridiculous
optimism evils that everybody knows to exist, it is equally
fatal to believe those evils irremediable. And with nations as with individuals, you must see them, understand
them, and, in a sense, love them, before you can expect
to mend them.

England would be mad indeed to shut her eyes to the
black cloud which overhangs Ireland, and the social upheaval now convulsing her from end to end. Her poverty,

some say, is at the root of this; and much of it is inevitable. Nothing could ever make her a rich country. Her inland stretches of green fertility are balanced by a barren rocky coast and leagues of mountain, moor, and bog; and her mild, moist climate, while adding to the outside beauty of the country, tends to enervate its already half-starved inhabitants. There is a well-known saying that an Irishman will work well anywhere—except in Ireland.

Then too—I own it with bitter regret, but I must own it—the whole country is, compared with England or Scotland, a full century behindhand in civilization. I do not speak of luxury, but of ordinary comfort—of making the best of whatever one has, of mending what wants repair, of removing what is unsightly, and adding to usefulness prettiness. All this seems to be totally absent from the ordinary Irish mind, except of course the cultivated classes, which are much the same in all countries. But the lower classes require to be taught the commonest things, exactly like children, and—who teaches them?

The gentry ought to do it—but do they? and moreover, where are they? Driven from or glad to quit a country which they find no temptation to remain in, only a limited portion of them can, will, or even dare live on their estates, so as to be at once a help and an example to their tenantry. The priests are the chief teachers left. Their influence is enormous, both for good and evil. Some are truly the fathers of their flock — knowing all their wants, sympathizing with all their miseries, and keeping them up to a standard of domestic purity which, as I have

said, is almost miraculous; beyond that of any other country in the world. And there are many priests who are
mere "firebrands;" low - born and half - educated, narrow
with the narrowness of ignorance, and fierce with unre-
strained passions; since if culture teaches nothing else, it
teaches self-control. These, instead of closing, only widen
the gulf between the upper and lower classes, so that
neither can understand the other. And England misun-
derstands both.

Yet, whatever outsiders may say or think, the Celtic
race is intrinsically a noble race; free from many modern
vices, even while clinging to some barbaric sins. You
may hate it, but you cannot despise it; and you cannot
live among it, even while seeing all its errors, without
feeling your heart warm to it, and to its enormous possibilities of good. If our legislators, ere dealing with Ireland, would first take the trouble to know Ireland, it would
be a curious study, well worth the pains of the new generation which will have to sit at Westminster.

The word brings to my mind an incident I saw this
year in a Westminster omnibus, just opposite the Houses
of Parliament. A little crippled girl was getting out
very feebly, all the other occupants of the vehicle looking on, but nobody doing anything, till a burly country-
man jumped out, saw her safe across the perilous street,
and on to the pavement, and returned to his seat. Somebody observed : "Poor little creature !"

"Ay," said the man, rather shamefaced at his own deed,
but still determined to brave it out. "But a 'andful of

'elp"—he had not an "h" in his vocabulary—"a 'andful of 'elp is worth a cartload of pity."

It is to put a similar idea into the heads and hearts of English people that I have written this book about Ireland.

THE END.

MISS MULOCK'S WORKS.

Among all modern novel-writers we place Miss Mulock first, not in genius, but in this, that with her the imagination is always employed for a high and noble purpose, and is always pure. We know of no modern novel-writer, and scarce of any writer of fiction of the past, whose works may be so safely commended as hers. But Miss Mulock never writes merely to amuse, nor yet to instruct, but always to elevate. Her very titles are themselves inspiriting—"A Noble Life," "A Life for a Life," "A Brave Lady," "The Woman's Kingdom." The ideals, as "John Halifax," and "A Brave Lady," are Christian ideals; and if she sometimes paints them in such perfection that we sigh at characterizations which appear to us to be unattainable, yet they are never less nor more than human. She never employs romance as a means of teaching theology, or even as an excuse for sermonizing. Her novels are the farthest possible removed from didactic stories. She inspires her readers simply by bringing them in contact with characters who are themselves inspiring, and the simple plots of her stories are only woven to give her an opportunity to describe her characters by their own conduct in seasons of trial. We cannot understand how one can arise from the perusal of any of her stories without being made better by the reading; and we believe the mother who wishes to guard her daughter against the sensational novel of the day will find in Miss Mulock's fiction a useful means to aid her in the accomplishment of her design.—*Illustrated Christian Weekly*, N. Y.

A BRAVE LADY. A Novel. Illustrated. 8vo, Paper, 60 cents; 12mo, Cloth, 90 cents.

A FRENCH COUNTRY FAMILY. From the French of Mme. DE WITT, *née* Guizot. Illustrated. 12mo, Cloth, $1 50.

AGATHA'S HUSBAND. A Novel. 8vo, Paper, 35 cents; 12mo, Illustrated, Cloth, 90 cents.

A HERO, and Other Tales. 12mo, Cloth, 90 cents.

A LEGACY: The Life and Remains of John Martin. Edited by Miss Mulock. 12mo, Cloth, 90 cents.

A LIFE FOR A LIFE. A Novel. 8vo, Paper, 40 cents; 12mo, Cloth, 90 cents.

A NOBLE LIFE. A Novel. 12mo, Cloth, 90 cents.

ABOUT MONEY, and Other Things. 12mo, Cloth, 90 cents.

AVILLION, and Other Tales. 8vo, Paper, 60 cents.

CHRISTIAN'S MISTAKE. A Novel. 12mo, Cloth, 90 cents.

FAIR FRANCE. 12mo, Cloth, $1 50.

HANNAH. A Novel. Illustrated. 8vo, Paper, 35 cents; 12mo, Cloth, 90 cents.

HIS LITTLE MOTHER, &c. 12mo, Cloth, 90 cents; 4to, Paper, 10 cents.

JOHN HALIFAX, GENTLEMAN. A Novel. 8vo, Paper, 50 cents; 12mo, Illustrated, Cloth, 90 cents; 4to, Paper, 15 cents.

KING ARTHUR. Not a Love-Story. 12mo, Paper, 25 cents; Cloth, 90 cents.

MISS TOMMY. A Mediæval Romance; And, In a House-boat. 12mo, Cloth, 90 cents; Paper, 50 cents.

MISTRESS AND MAID. A Household Story. 8vo, Paper, 30 cents; 12mo, Cloth, 90 cents.

MOTHERLESS; or, A Parisian Family. From the French of Mme. DE WITT, *née* Guizot. For Girls in their Teens. Illustrated. 12mo, Cloth, $1 50.

MY MOTHER AND I. A Love-Story. Illustrated. 8vo, Paper, 40 cents; 12mo, Cloth, 90 cents.

NOTHING NEW. Tales. 8vo, Paper, 30 cents.

OLIVE. A Novel. 8vo, Paper, 35 cents; 12mo, Illustrated, Cloth, 90 cents.

OUR YEAR. Illustrated. 16mo, Cloth, $1 00.

PLAIN SPEAKING. 12mo, Cloth, 90 cents; 4to, Paper, 15 cents.

SERMONS OUT OF CHURCH. 12mo, Cloth, 90 cents.

SONGS OF OUR YOUTH. Set to Music. Square 4to, Cloth, $2 50.

STUDIES FROM LIFE. A Novel. 12mo, Cloth, 90 cents.

THE ADVENTURES OF A BROWNIE. As told to my Child. Illustrated. Square 16mo, Cloth, 90 cents.

THE FAIRY BOOK. The Best Popular Fairy Stories rendered anew. Illustrated. 12mo, Cloth, 90 cents.

THE HEAD OF THE FAMILY. A Novel. 8vo, Paper, 50 cents; 12mo, Illustrated, Cloth, 90 cents.

THE LAUREL BUSH. An Old-fashioned Love-Story. Illustrated. 8vo, Paper, 25 cents; 12mo, Cloth, 90 cents.

THE LITTLE LAME PRINCE. Illustrated. Square 16mo, Cloth, $1 00.

THE OGILVIES. A Novel. 8vo, Paper, 35 cents; 12mo, Illustrated, Cloth, 90 cents.

THE UNKIND WORD, and Other Stories. 12mo, Cloth, 90 cents.

THE UNKNOWN COUNTRY. Illustrated. 8vo, Cloth. (*Just Ready.*)

THE WOMAN'S KINGDOM. A Love-Story. Illustrated. 8vo, Paper, 60 cents; 12mo, Cloth, 90 cents.

TWO MARRIAGES. John Bowerbank's Wife and Parson Garland's Daughter. 12mo, Cloth, 90 cents.

YOUNG MRS. JARDINE. A Novel. 4to, Paper, 10 cents; 12mo, Cloth, 90 cents.

BOOKS FOR GIRLS.

Written or Edited by the Author of "John Halifax." 16mo, Cloth, 90 cents each.

1. LITTLE SUNSHINE'S HOLIDAY. A Picture from Life. By Miss MULOCK. With Illustrations by Frölich.

2. THE COUSIN FROM INDIA. By GEORGIANA M. CRAIK. Illustrated.

3. TWENTY YEARS AGO. From the Journal of a Girl in her Teens. Edited by Miss MULOCK. With an Illustration.

4. IS IT TRUE? Tales, Curious and Wonderful, collected by Miss MULOCK. With an Illustration.

5. AN ONLY SISTER. By Madame DE WITT. With six Illustrations.

6. MISS MOORE. By GEORGIANA M. CRAIK. Illustrated.

HARPER'S LIBRARY EDITION OF MISS MULOCK'S WORKS.

12mo, Cloth, 90 cents per volume; $24 30 per set; Half Calf, $67 50.

A BRAVE LADY.

A HERO.

A LEGACY.

A LIFE FOR A LIFE.

A NOBLE LIFE.

ABOUT MONEY, AND OTHER THINGS.

AGATHA'S HUSBAND.

CHRISTIAN'S MISTAKE

HANNAH.

HIS LITTLE MOTHER, &c.

JOHN HALIFAX.

KING ARTHUR.

MISS TOMMY.

MISTRESS AND MAID.

MY MOTHER AND I.

OLIVE.

PLAIN SPEAKING.

SERMONS OUT OF CHURCH.

STUDIES FROM LIFE.

THE FAIRY BOOK.

THE HEAD OF THE FAMILY.

THE LAUREL BUSH.

THE OGILVIES.

THE UNKIND WORD.

THE WOMAN'S KINGDOM.

TWO MARRIAGES.

YOUNG MRS. JARDINE.

PUBLISHED BY HARPER & BROTHERS, NEW YORK.

☞ *Any of the above works sent by mail, postage prepaid, to any part of the United States or Canada, on receipt of the price.*